PRINCESS
OF THE DARK

Taniquelle Tulipano

A *Bella Tulip* Book
First published in the United Kingdom by Bella Tulip Publishing
2016

© Copyright Taniquelle Tulipano 2016

Cover design © Copyright Francessca Webster,
Francessca's Romance Reviews 2016
Book Cover Image © Refat Mamutov 2016

PRINCESS OF THE DARK

Paperback 9780993562662
Kindle 9780993562679
ePub 9780993562686

Editing/Proofreading Rebecca Weeks, Rebecca's editing services

Book formatted by Taniquelle Tulipano

Bella Tulip Publishing
83 Ducie Street
Manchester
M1 2JQ

www.bellatulippublishing.com

Words cannot tell you how much I love you.
This is for you D.

PROLOGUE 7

CHAPTER ONE 8

CHAPTER TWO 20

CHAPTER THREE 26

CHAPTER FOUR 33

CHAPTER FIVE 38

CHAPTER SIX 42

CHAPTER SEVEN 45

CHAPTER EIGHT 50

CHAPTER NINE 56

CHAPTER TEN 60

CHAPTER ELEVEN 67

CHAPTER TWELVE 75

CHAPTER THIRTEEN 80

CHAPTER FOURTEEN 85

CHAPTER FIFTEEN 91

CHAPTER SIXTEEN 98

CHAPTER SEVENTEEN 101

CHAPTER EIGHTEEN 104

CHAPTER NINETEEN 108

CHAPTER TWENTY 111

CHAPTER TWENTY-ONE..117

CHAPTER TWENTY-TWO...122

CHAPTER TWENTY-THREE...130

CHAPTER TWENTY-FOUR 136

CHAPTER TWENTY-FIVE...138

CHAPTER TWENTY-SIX 144

CHAPTER TWENTY-SEVEN 150

CHAPTER TWENTY-EIGHT...158

CHAPTER TWENTY-NINE 163

CHAPTER THIRTY 171

CHAPTER THIRTY-ONE...174

CHAPTER THIRTY-TWO..182

CHAPTER THIRTY-THREE 192

CHAPTER THIRTY-FOUR 197

CHAPTER THIRTY-FIVE..201

PROLOGUE

Once upon a time there lived a man who took his life for granted. He knew of the various dangers that had afflicted people he knew but never did he think anything would happen to him. One day, two monsters burst into his world and stole the life he had away from him. Soon the man discovered that he was no longer a man, but a monster. It was not long before he started to grieve over the life he had lost. No matter how hard he had tried, he could not get it back. Time got its hands on the monster and the years blurred into each other. Slowly the monster's humanity ebbed away until there was all but none left. There was just enough to keep him from being completely heartless.

That man was me, that monster was me. My path changed when the most amazing woman burst into my existence and made me feel alive for the first time in over two hundred years. But happiness is not designed to last forever. Fate is not done with me yet. It took my life but it is not happy with just that. It is greedy, it wants more. It now has a new target in its sight and it will stop at nothing to get it. I must fight like I have never fought before or all will be truly lost.

CHAPTER ONE

Raphael

Until a short while ago my life was uncomplicated. Even though it was not much, I knew what my calling was. I drank blood, I toyed with whatever females I wanted, and I killed criminals for sport. Everything was fine until I came across a particular woman called Rosannah. What started off as a normal conquest turned into something quite bizarre.

I made up a story that I needed Rosannah to evaluate my home. Everything was fine and then Harry, a skivvy nobody of The Synod, turned up and skewed my judgement. One moment of idiocy, I allowed my anger to get the better of me, and Rosannah saw my true nature. I had wanted her to see my true nature, but much later. Under normal circumstances I would have brainwashed her to forget what she had seen and I could have carried on with my plan. But brainwashing did not work on her and as a result, I had to keep her hostage to keep the secret of our kind safe.

While I had Rosannah captive, a human called Alex had turned up to take her under the guise of trying to rescue her. After torturing him, it soon became apparent that he was being controlled by a vampire and had been brainwashed into not remembering anything about their plans, as well as who and what was controlling him. I had Lawrence keep an eye on him in the hopes that we might find out more information. The most we managed to learn about

Alex's situation was that two or more vampires were controlling him with voice distorters via telephone.

Rosannah's captivity was short lived and I had to throw her out because of Nicholas and his moment of madness. I panicked and acted irrationally, but once it was done there wasn't much I could do about it. In order to keep The Synod content, I erased any evidence of Rosannah ever being at my house. I had Lawrence keep an eye on Alex once he came back from following Nicholas to Chile and getting Nicholas to admit himself to the Chile V Retreat, a vampire mental health clinic. Even though my heart was broken, the situation was going well, that was up until Lawrence revealed that Alex was back on the scene, pretending to take Rosannah on dates. I charged Evangeline with helping Lawrence keep an eye on Alex after Lawrence's failure.

I had no choice but to enter Rosannah's life once again. I knew it would have only been a matter of time before I did, but with Alex trying to do God knows what it gave me the perfect excuse to get involved sooner. Our reunion was bumpy to say the least, but everything was back on track until it was revealed that my dear brother, Nicholas, had left the clinic early, and had come back. Then brainwashed Rosannah's best friend, Brianna, into a relationship with him and fooled Rosannah into thinking he was a human called Michael. Whilst Brianna was oblivious it was quite the shock to the rest of us, but especially hard on Rosannah. Lawrence had pulled me away from Rosannah to tell me that Alex was getting an instructional phone call.

We staked outside Alex's home, but all that we heard was an odd jumbled sentence. Alex left his home and we followed. He was up to something and we hoped that he would lead us to those responsible. After a while it became apparent that he was not actually going anywhere in particular and it dawned on me that he was leading Lawrence and I on a wild goose chase. The purpose was clear: to leave Rosannah unattended. I let the thought of finally finding out who was controlling Alex blind me from seeing what was truly happening. My stupidity had put Rosannah in danger. I raced back to Rosannah's flat with Lawrence in tow and that is where we are now.

Using the key I had cut, I let us in. My eyes dark to the crumpled up rug on the floor and an involuntary growl escapes my lips at the evidence of her abduction. Lawrence races off to check the rooms and Marmalade peeps her head out from behind the couch.

"I am sorry," I whisper as I crouch down. She slowly comes out and makes her way over to me. I hold my hands out to her and she jumps into my arms and head butts my chest while purring. I stroke behind her ears as Lawrence reappears.

"She's not here, let's head back to yours to see if she's there," Lawrence says.

Lawrence's words slam into me and my mind goes into overload.

"We both know that she is not there. Vampires would only need minutes to take Rosannah and we spent more than enough time following Alex. They are long gone but I will not give up," I say.

"It's worth a try Raph," Lawrence murmurs.

"I do not think it is. We must figure out who's behind all of this. I know who *could* have her and they will not be at my house." I whisper, not wanting to say his name out loud for fear of it being true.

"Who do you think has her?" Lawrence asks.

"Nicholas," I admit.

"There's no way Raph. You and I both know he's not capable of orchestrating all of this. Nicholas controlling Alex? I don't think so," Lawrence says, his brow creasing.

"Is he really the brother we always thought he was? He has spent the last God knows how long brainwashing Brianna into a relationship, so he can what? Spy on Rosannah and God knows what else," I say.

"I know Raph, but this isn't Nicholas and deep down you know it." He places a hand on my shoulder. "We all have our bad days, although it seems like Nicholas has had a whole bunch of them at once," he confesses.

"I damn well hope for his sake he is not behind any of this, but with or without you, I am going to see him!"

"Why don't you calm down first? Doesn't Rosannah have neighbours? We could ask them if they saw anything," Lawrence suggests. I am not keen on wasting time but he may be on to something. I don't even know where Nicholas lives and if we only manage to his address, it would be worth it.

"We will ask Brianna's mother; she lives immediately below Rosannah's flat. We will ask her some questions and get Nicholas's address."

Lawrence looks like he is about to argue, but I do not wait to find out. I dash off and he follows. I knock on the front door of the flat below and an older version of Brianna answers.

I watch as she takes the sight of Lawrence and I in. Slowly she looks us up and down, stopping momentarily on our crotches. Revulsion comes to mind. It is obvious that she finds us attractive. Her cheeks blush, her eyes dilate, and her lips curve into a small smile.

"How can I help you?" She coos.

"My name is Raphael and this is my brother Lawrence. We are looking for someone," I reply.

"Well, I'd say you've found them," she grins. I look to Lawrence who is smirking and mentally curse him.

"What's your name?" I ask turning back to Brianna's mother.

"Nora."

"Nora, I am looking for my girlfriend," a playful grin spreads across her face. "Before you absentmindedly open your mouth, you will never be my girlfriend." I say turning on my charm as I brainwash her. I look at Lawrence who is trying not to laugh. "Whatever it is you're thinking, stop at once," I say to him. Lawrence ignores me and looks to Nora.

"Do you know much of what goes on in this building?" He asks, brainwashing her himself.

"Oh, I know everything that goes on here," she answers. This doesn't surprise me. She looks like someone who would be happy to stuff her nose up...

"So you hear who comes and goes to Rosannah's apartment?" Lawrence asks, breaking my train of thought.

"Oh yes, *come* being the operative word," she laughs. It turns out it is still possible for a person's personality to shine through when being brainwashed, unfortunately. "There's a man who visits her regularly." She continues. "I've never seen him but I hear what they get up to sometimes," she says with a grin. Horror befalls me and I turn to Lawrence who looks like a kid in a sweet shop.

"Is that so?" He asks with a raised eyebrow.

"Yes. When Cody has been in bed and I've heard Rosannah at it I've had a really good masturbation session. It's happened on a few occasions," she admits. Lawrence bursts out laughing. I stare at him wide eyed while he laughs his head off for about ten minutes. Once he calms down he looks at me.

"That was hilarious!" he exclaims. Knowing that this woman has pleasured herself while I have made love to Rosannah makes my skin crawl.

"I can never un-hear that."

"Why would you want to?" Lawrence asks chuckling and he turns to Nora. "Now you can put a face to the guy you hear banging away above you," he says pointing a thumb at me. "Anything else you want to get off of your chest?"

"Lawrence!" I warn him but it's too late.

"You two will certainly star the next time I flick the bean. You are both drop dead gorgeous," she admits while she's still under the influence of Lawrence's brainwashing.

"If only you knew the half of it," Lawrence flirts. I punch Lawrence in the arm faster than Nora can register. "I think Raphael here would love to hear anything else you may have to say," he says and sidesteps away from me.

"I hate you," I whisper to him as Nora starts talking, until she is cut off by Lawrence's reply.

"Such anger Raphael. I think you have a problem."

"Yes, it's called Lawrence," I say through gritted teeth. "Have you seen anyone visit Rosannah today?" I ask Nora.

"Yes, it was really weird. My daughter's boyfriend, Michael, visited her. You know, you *really* look like him. Are you sure you're not him? It's quite freaky just how similar you are," she says pointing to Lawrence.

Lawrence and I look at each other.

"Please elaborate," I order her.

"I don't just hear things; I look out of my spy hole too."

"That's what she said," jokes Lawrence.

"Oh, naughty," she smiles at Lawrence and playfully slaps his shoulder.

"You don't know the meaning of naughty until..."

"Lawrence! For god's sake behave yourself. I really can't take you anywhere," I chastise him.

"Now how boring would that be?" He asks.

"Whenever I hear footsteps I look out," Nora says pulling us back to her.

"You really need to get a life," I mutter to myself as Nora continues, oblivious to my comment.

"About two hours ago Michael went to see Rosannah. I found it a little strange but I thought maybe he wanted to ask Brianna to marry him and wanted to discuss it with Rosannah. They are best friends after all."

"Could you hear them at all?" Lawrence asks. Finally, something sensible comes out of his mouth!

"Michael went up there and they had a conversation that made no sense," she says scrunching her face up.

"What the hell does that mean?" I yell.

"Well, Rosannah kept calling him Nicholas and they discussed him discharging himself from a clinic and about some plan he had been carrying out. I found it a little disturbing and I've been pondering whether to tell Brianna about it," she admits.

"Where do Brianna and Michael live?" I ask her. My brother's fake name feels like fire on my tongue.

"Hold on, I will get my address book. I don't remember it off by heart," she says and goes off. Now that is a surprise. After a few minutes she returns and hands me an open pink and purple flowery book. I memorize the address and hand the book back.

"Put the book away and return to me," I order. She does as she's told and comes back. "You will forget everything that has happened over the past three hours. Is anyone else here?"

"My son Cody is here but he's been asleep all day. He's been really ill with the flu," she says. Satisfied that it is only Nora I need to give a new story to, I continue.

"For the past three hours you've watched telly but I visited you to ask if you knew where Rosannah was. You did not know but you said you would tell her that her boyfriend was looking for her," I say and go to the door. I stop myself as something else comes to mind. "And please, for the love of God, stop masturbating to the sounds that come from Rosannah's apartment. It is beyond disturbing," I walk out and race off down the street. Lawrence joins me with a smirk on his face.

"It may be disturbing to you but it's funny as hell to me!" he laughs.

"Do not mention this to me ever again. It's going to take god knows how long for my skin to stop crawling. I am going to see Nicholas. Because you are concerned Rosannah may turn up at mine you can head back to mine in case she turns up," I tell him.

"Raphael, I would really like to see Nicholas too," he says with a slight frown. I forget how attached brothers are to one another and I feel somewhat guilty that I have neglected to see how Lawrence may be holding up with all of this.

"I am very doubtful but what if she does actually turn up at mine?" I ask putting on a front.

Lawrence gets out his phone and dials. Within seconds a high-pitched whiny voice answers.

"What do you want?" Evangeline whinges down the line.

"Can you get over to Raphs?" he asks her.

"Raph sent me home. I'm not coming back now," she whines.

"Rosannah is missing!" he yells.

"What do you mean missing?" she asks.

My patience is wearing incredibly thin. Rosannah is missing and wasting time with Brianna's mother has used it all up. I grab the phone from Lawrence.

"Look, enough time has been wasted. Lawrence and I were led on a wild goose chase by Alex. In the meantime, Rosannah has gone missing. Can you PLEASE get over to my house in case Rosannah turns up there?" I order.

"Wow, no need to shout. I'm on my way to yours," she sulks and the line goes dead. I hand the phone back to Lawrence.

"You always have such a knack with her," Lawrence says.

"It is all in the delivery of the words," I say with a shrug.

With Lawrence by my side we head to Nicholas and Brianna's apartment. I knock at the door and Brianna answers. "Go into your bedroom and stay there until I tell you to come back out," I instruct her before she has the chance to say anything. She smiles and walks off happily. We enter to see Nicholas sat on the couch.

"Oh Lawrence, I came to see you but you weren't in," he says to him but as he claps eyes on me I see red. I storm over to him and hold him up by his throat.

"Where is she?!" I yell at him. I watch the confusion on his face slowly turn into realisation.

"She should be at home," he says as he hangs there. My grip on his throat is tight, it would crush a human and kill them, but not Nicholas. I can feel his muscles move with ease beneath my palm as he talks.

"Try again!"

"Can you put me down so I can talk to you on ground level please?" he asks. Lawrence puts his hand on my arm and my anger abates a little. I place Nicholas back down and he straightens himself out.

"I left her safe and sound in her flat," he says, confirming Nora's recollection of seeing him earlier.

"If you have hurt her so help me!" I threaten.

"You'll what? There's isn't much you can do!" he yells. "Plus, no matter what you think I didn't hurt her at all. I went to see her so we could talk. We had a heart to heart and put things to rest. It's the truth."

"You better pray that you have told me the truth," I tell him.

"I don't know what this is even all about. Yeah, I'd brainwashed Rosannah's best friend into a relationship so I could get closer to her. Not only have I realised how stupid my plan was but I also realised I wasn't in love with Rosannah. I just thought I was. Brianna is really growing on me to be honest. I thought it was a good idea to clear the air, seeing as I haven't actually done anything to Rosannah."

"Well, courtesy of Alex's vampire puppet master, Rosannah is now missing. Alex led us on a wild goose chase and when we finally realised that we raced over to Rosannah's apartment to find her gone," I say.

"So you thought it was me?" he asks.

"Can you blame me?" I reply.

"No, I don't. What can I do to help?" Nicholas asks, sounding genuinely concerned.

"You want to help? Find her Nicholas," I say. Lawrence steps in front of me facing Nicholas.

"Look, if you want to help why don't you come with me and..."

"I will head out to Mathias to tell him what's happened." I interrupt and dash off. We are at a dead end and I hope that maybe Mathias has learned something new.

I am there in minutes and Mathias opens the door as I arrive.

"What do I owe the pleasure of your visit dear boy?" he asks as he follows me into his kitchen.

"The bastards have taken Rosannah," I say and turn to face him.

CHAPTER TWO

Rosannah

"You," I whisper. The word is painful to get out and is barely audible, but I know the vampire I'm looking up at can hear me.

"Oh poor little Rosannah. Are you *really* that surprised?" Reggie sneers at me.

"Maybe it's ridiculous to be surprised that *you'd* do something like this, but *him*?" I say as I point at a freshly turned Harry. "I'm utterly shocked. I never saw that coming."

"It will come as no surprise that I have wanted to screw Raphael over for years, but Harry here was particularly eager to be involved. Why turn down help when it's so willing to do anything you want?" Reggie smiles pleasantly at me. I feel sick to my stomach.

"I can see he's been rewarded for his efforts," I say in disgust. Harry's light grey eyes flash darker in recognition.

"How could you do this Reggie?" I sob. It's a stupid question, but the pain inside forces me to ask.

"The question isn't how, although it's pretty obvious, I'm a VAMPIRE. So, the question is *why*." He moves in closer to me. He waits for my question.

"Why?" I ask simply, backing away from him slightly, but he backs up and turns away from me.

"We both know that I don't like you very much. That's being too kind, I don't like you at all and add to that the fact you can't be brainwashed you are the single biggest threat and liability to the entire vampire population. Not even taking my personal feelings towards you into account, you should have been terminated as soon as your aversion to my kind was discovered, but Raphael was having none of it. You see, that's what happens when one thinks with their dick instead of their head. I suppose for those who are unintelligent it's easy to confuse which head is for what." He says thoughtfully before turning back to me. "I don't even understand why Raphael is so attached to you. To be quite honest it appals me. You're a human and a very unattractive one at that. You're meant to be fed on, not lusted after and fucked."

Harry stifles a laugh but Reggie ignores him and carries on. "A human who cannot be brainwashed is a very worrisome thing. The Synod isn't too bothered by it when they should be, and for some godforsaken reason, Mathias always panders to Raphael. *That,* I have never understood. It's like Mathias left his balls behind with his humanity. Either that, or he has a penchant for your dear *boyfriend*." He spits. "I want you to know that I am not the only one who wants shot of you. There are numerous people who want you gone. So far they have been all mouth and no trousers and someone had to step up to the plate, but you see this isn't just about some silly flesh bag who can blab to the world about our existence. It's a part of it yes, but there are issues that go back years. Hundreds of years." He says. What the hell is he talking about? I asked for an explanation and now I'm very confused. Reggie must have picked up on it because he flashes me a gloating smile.

"How can this, whatever it is, go back that far?" I ask.

"You see; I was one of the vampires who killed Raphael's family." I gasp, which cuts him off. "Oh come now, don't look so shocked. That's only the tip of the iceberg. I had some help you know."

"From who?"

"Ah, now wouldn't it be nice and easy if I answered all of your questions? Well guess what? I'm not going to just give you the answers you want. Think of it like you and sweet Raphael, when you two met. You were a good girl. Oh, you certainly wanted to be a naughty girl but you didn't let Raphael get his meat hooks into you straight away did you? You made him wait, teased him. Then sent him over the edge. I'm very much the same. You can have a little peak but no viewing my tartars until I'm ready." He says, his voice full of sarcasm. I have no idea why I'm so shocked by his words and demeanour. He's nasty, creepy and doesn't care at all, but it still hits hard. Even though this hurts I want to know more about Raphael and Reggie and fortunately my mouth continues to work.

"Why did you murder Raphael's family?" I ask. If I get out of this alive, I want to tell Raphael as much as I can.

"It was just fun and games. I went along with it for the laugh. There is more to this story but spoilers are like candy. Too many will make you sick," He sneers and something flashes behind his eyes.

"Did *you* change Raphael?" I ask. I might be able to at least give Raphael closure on that.

"Maybe I did, maybe I didn't, but you don't need to worry your little head about that. All you need to know is that it was agreed he would be changed but all along I had planned to go against my word. I was going to see to it that he would be killed and betray the trust that had been bestowed upon me, but I changed my mind. Why did I change my mind yet again? Let's say I had a change of heart." He says. I sit open mouthed. Seven words hammer against my brain. *It was agreed he would be changed.* Don't tell me Raphael *wanted* to be a vampire, *arranged* to be a vampire. He doesn't think that he was murdered. It would make sense if *he* was behind his transition.

"It was agreed he would be changed? You mean Raphael *agreed*?" I ask, my voice going up in pitch. I don't *want* to know the answer but I *have* to know.

"Oh good Heavens no, don't be so stupid! At the time it was the worst thing that could have happened to him, from his perspective anyway. Look at him now though, flourishing like the pathetic moron he is."

"Don't you feel any kind of remorse?!" I yell at him. He raises an eyebrow and leans towards Harry.

"I don't think she understands that I do not care about other people, human or vampire," he says to him. Harry grins like a Cheshire cat as Reggie comes over and crouches down in front of me. I back up until I hit the wall, but Reggie edges closer until he's only a few inches away from me. "My *dear*, I used to be an incredibly compassionate human being. I was a holy man and spent my every waking hour helping as many people in as many ways as I possibly could. I was on my way to an early death with the lack of sleep and all of the stress that I so willingly asked people to place on my shoulders. That was over *two thousand years ago*. Now tell me, smart ass, what do you think time has done to that compassion?" He asks.

"A holy man? *You* were a holy man?"

"It's typical that you would only hone in on that," He says as he stands up and walks away from me. "Harry, will you go and shut that noise up please! That incessant whinging is pressing on me." Incessant noise? If I exclude Harry and Reggie, the only other noise around here is me talking! I panic, but Harry races out of the door, leaving it open. I eye it, but I know that I won't be able to even move before Reggie would stop me. Harry returns, closing the door behind him.

"It's done," he says. What or who did Harry *shut up*? A shiver travels down my spine. Reggie appears lost in thought and while he's distracted, I take in my surroundings.

We are in a rounded bricked room that narrows the further up it goes. The ceiling is beyond what I can see and the floor is concrete, cold and harsh like the vampire's in here with me. A single light bulb hangs from suspended wires and broken tables and chairs lay discarded and scattered around. I can't think of a tower, like this, that is anywhere near where I live. This must be far from home.

"Yes, Yes!" Reggie yells, pulling me out of my thoughts. He suddenly stops and turns to face me. "I used to be a holy man. My time was the God's, my life was the God's, and my *soul* was the God's. I lived and breathed to do the God's work. The fact that

I was a servant to the God's may be quite a surprise to you. All you see before you is a creature who is devoid of compassion, but once I was human and a VERY decent one at that. This is a pill that is hard for you to swallow because your human brain cannot truly comprehend being on this Earth for over two thousand years, nor can it fully understand what long periods of time can do to the wants and desires of the mind." Reggie has a point. How can I even begin to imagine what it would be like to exist for *thousands* of years? I have no idea what it I will be like in sixty years, if I make it that long. A sinking feeling settles in my stomach. Reggie maybe talking philosophically to me now, but I remind myself that he's brought me here for a purpose. What is that purpose?

CHAPTER THREE

Lawrence

"So we've traced Alex's movements to this phone box from where you and Raph left him, and there's no sign of him asides from the very light scent that leads here," says Nicholas in frustration.

"I knew it wouldn't lead to much, but it was worth a shot," I reply and shrug.

"If we're here, where's Evangeline? Or did he keep her out of this? He'd be an idiot to in a situation like this."

"She's waiting at Raphael's in case Rosannah turns up." I reply.

"So why isn't anyone stationed at Rosannah's?"

"Raphael put Nora in charge of that," I say. Nicholas laughs.

"That woman is probably the most unreliable person I have ever met! Are you happy to carry on trying to track Alex by yourself? It's best if one of us is there and I volunteer to go. I can pop home on the way and tell Brianna that she can come out of the bedroom," he says.

"You know Raphael needs to tell her," I remind him. I don't know what possessed him to instruct her to wait in the bedroom until *he* told her she could return. He obviously isn't thinking clearly at all, but love will do that to you, I would know.

"I'll tell her Raphael told me to tell her, failing that I'll have to phone him and get him to tell her down the phone," he says. I really do wish the first option would work as I can't see Raphael being too pleased about Nicholas going to Rosannah's on his own, but I know it won't. "Keep in touch," He says as he dashes off.

I sniff around the phone box for a while. There was a faint scent that led to here, but judging by the scent that lingers here and doesn't lead off anywhere, I can deduce that Alex called someone from here. It must have been a vampire who collected him. Scents are a funny thing, if there is little to no wind, vampires can trace smells, but vampires can use their speed to cover their tracks making it hard for us to sniff out each other or any human they are carrying. I'm not going to find out much here, so I decide to head back to Alex's home.

When I arrive at Alex's home I carefully and discreetly break in and discover that the place is in a state of disarray. It was fine when Raphael and I were here earlier and the strange thing bit is that it hasn't been ransacked, things have just been randomly thrown around. An uneasy feeling settles over me. Why would the vampires that control him come back here, with or without him, and throw his stuff around? Even if they had brought him here, why would they do this and then take him elsewhere? It doesn't make any sense, but hanging around here is pointless. In light of recent events I doubt he will be returning anytime soon. Unfortunately, I can't follow where they may have taken Alex so I decide to join Nicholas.

I dash off and I'm with him within minutes. Nicholas is standing inside Rosannah's flat with the door wide open. I walk straight in.

27

"Something really bizarre is going...." I stop midsentence at the sight in front of me. Nicholas is standing by the window with a cat in his arms. He's tenderly stroking it. This has to be one of the strangest things I have ever seen. Nicholas *hates* cats. He had the worst allergy when we were human which turned into a deep hatred. Even though the allergy went when he became a vampire, the hate stayed. As a result, cats would always detect his dislike of them and in return they would hiss and on a few occasions would even attack him whether he paid them attention or not.

However, this cat seems to love Nicholas. I compose myself and start again. "Something really bizarre is going on. I could only trace Alex to that phone box. I determined that he must have called someone to collect him so I went back to his place to see if I could shed any light on what's going on. What I found were possessions randomly thrown around. The place was fine when Raphael and I followed Alex from there earlier."

"Could it not have been a ransacking or struggle?" He asks.

"It didn't look like it," I shake my head.

"That is strange. There's nothing to report this end," Nicholas says as he strokes Rosannah's cat. The cat is purring in immense appreciation. Something then occurs to me.

"How did you get in here?" I ask and regret the question immediately. I can see the accusation in his eyes. I didn't mean it like that but Nicholas composes himself.

"Nora has a key. Rosannah has locked herself out a few times and her mother hasn't helped so Rosannah gave Nora a key. Well, that's what Nora has said. You and I both know she was probably given one because someone needed to look after the cat while Raphael held Rosannah hostage. He wasn't going to look after the cat himself, but she means something to Rosannah, and so that meant something to him. I should have realised then that he had a soft spot for Rosannah," he admits.

"Talking about Rosannah..." I start. "I must ask about...your recent actions," I say carefully. I don't want Nicholas to misinterpret my intentions. He's my brother and I care about him.

"I thought this would come," he admits and turns around. "I'm so sorry brother. I should never have done any of the things I did. I have no idea what I was thinking. I was just jealous of what they had. Rosannah is Raphael's and if I hadn't had been so blind, I would have seen that."

"Were you also blind when you discharged yourself from the clinic, came here, took on a new identity and brainwashed Rosannah's best friend just to have a chance with Rosannah?" I ask, raising an eyebrow.

"Yes. Very blind." He frowns.

"You should be ashamed," I say. Nicholas's eyes widen a little, it's a sign that he is. I haven't seen this reaction from my brother in a very, very long time. No matter how small the reaction I am incredibly glad to see it. "You want to know what hurts the most about all of this? You never once spoke to me about it. You could have come to me at any point in time but you didn't."

"I knew you would try to talk me out of my plans and all of the feelings I thought I had. I really should have spoken to you about it and for that I couldn't be sorry enough," he says sadly.

"You're not the only one, I am too. I should have seen what was going on with you. If I had, then none of this...."

"It's not your fault. I hid it well," He interrupts.

"That you did." I force a smile. We have always been so in tuned with one another. We know how the other is feeling and what's on the others mind. This is the first time it hasn't happened.

"I feel so awful about all of this, it will be hard to gain the trust I lost," he frowns. "But, I am happy to be back with the family again." I walk over and half man-hug him. The cat protests a little, but once I let go of Nicholas the cat's happy again.

"We're okay, Evangeline won't realise what you've done is actually really bad because we both know she's not all quite there. With Raphael and Rosannah, they will come around soon enough, I'm sure." I say with a hopeful smile.

"I hope you're right," he says as he lightly scratches behind the cat's ears making her purr.

"So, are you going to end things with Rosannah's friend?" I ask him.

"No," he says, lightly shaking his head.

"Nicholas, you can't keep leading her on," I warn.

"It was a means to an end but I really like her," he says simply and shrugs his shoulders.

"Really?" I ask with a smile.

"Yes, she's actually pretty okay," he says. Could it be my brother really likes a girl? *Loves* her even? I leave it there because I don't want to push him too much but I will keep an eye on him.

"I really should phone Raphael to let him know our findings, or lack thereof rather," I say, changing the subject as I get my phone out. I call Raphael and he answers instantly.

"Yes," he demands.

"Oh, hi Lawrence how are you? Why I'm fine Raphael, thank you for asking," I reply.

"Just tell me why you have called me," he says deadpan.

"You can be such an ass you know, but I'm sure you already know that." Raphael sighs impatiently down the line. "Okay, I'll get on with it. I determined Alex was collected by a vampire from a phone box that wasn't too far from where we left him. I went back to his place and it had been turned over. No sign of Rosannah or Alex there. I didn't think he would be coming home any time soon so Nicholas and I are now at Rosannah's," I tell him.

"Why did you let Nicholas go off?" Raphael asks.

"Ah, he had to call you didn't he?" I had forgotten about that.

"Yes he did."

"Look, we can't persecute Nicholas forever, he did something wrong and he's sorry. He's tried his best to put it right."

"I am not persecuting him anymore. I was simply wondering why he went off on his own," he says softly. I sigh in relief. It sounds to me like he could have forgiven Nicholas too.

"Oh, well...he thought it would be best if someone checked out Rosannah's place." I tell him.

"But Brianna's mother was doing that!" he yells down the line.

"Nicholas was concerned about Nora. Apparently she isn't very reliable."

"I can believe that," he says with a sigh.

"What do you want us to do now?" I ask.

"You have a choice. You can either stay there to see if she turns up or you can go and keep Evangeline company."

"We'll stay here" I say quickly.

"I thought you would say that," Raphael says before hanging up. Nicholas goes and closes the front door and walks over to the couch. He puts the cat down on the windowsill and it complains with a hiss. As soon as Nicholas sits down on the couch the cat jumps onto his lap. It walks around in a few circles, kneading Nicholas's lap with its claws. Once it's satisfied, it lies down, curls up, and starts purring again. I shake my head slowly in surprise.

CHAPTER FOUR

Rosannah

Reggie has been pacing for some time now. It's as if he's trying to figure out what to do. He stops suddenly which makes me jump.

"I really should do what's been agreed, but I want to deviate," Reggie admits with an evil grin.

"No matter what you have planned, Raphael will find me," I tell him. He looks at me thoughtfully.

"I'm sure he's trying his best to find you, but I can assure you that he will be too late. I have done everything I can to throw him off the trail. He will find you when I want him to find you," he tells me.

"You're wrong, he'll find me in time," I say defiantly.

"You really think the sun shines out of his ass, don't you?" he asks. I raise my eyebrows. "He's not a saint Rosannah. He's a monster, just like me. His idea of fun is to take women like you and brainwash his way into their panties. Sometimes he has waited to brainwash *after* the event."

"I know that Raphael *used* to be a monster, and I also know that his past behaviour has something to do with coming to terms with his immortality, something that was forced upon him. Even though anything he has done in the past can never be fully excused, I know that he lost sight of who he really was. A vampire can change just like a person can. If I make it out of here alive, I will forgive him for everything he has ever done because that's the greatest thing anyone can do and I will do it for him because I love him!"

"I'm beginning to get quite bored. Harry, go fetch the other one." Good God, who else could he have here?

Harry races off once more, but when he returns, he's not alone.

"Alex!" I yell as Harry hands him over to Reggie.

"Did you make it look like his place was ransacked?" Reggie asks Harry, ignoring me.

"It will be okay," Alex says to me, but I can see the fear in his eyes.

"No one will ever be able to tell it was faked." He smiles. Why the hell would they do that? Is that supposed to throw Raphael off of the trail? Raphael will find me in no time at all. Suddenly, a sickening crack echoes around the chamber, ricocheting off of the walls, and Alex lays on the floor on his front with his head facing upwards at a very unnatural angle. I gasp and hold back from gagging as the realisation washes over me. Alex is dead.

"I am a vampire; do you think I can change? Feel like forgiving me for everything I have ever done? For nearly severing Alex's head when I shattered his neck?" Reggie asks me. I stare up in horror as I fight against wanting to throw up. "No, I didn't think so. All your talk about forgiveness was a load of bullshit. You're happy to forgive Raphael because you love him and I can only presume he never forced you into his bed without you gagging for it! Even if he did, you would be stupid enough to still drool at his feet! Not only are you biased and incredibly dense, you are a complete and utter hypocrite. What makes you think that *anything* you say to me will have any effect on me whatsoever? I don't really listen to anyone but I know that anything you have to say isn't worth the breath you'd waste on it!" He yells. I'm still in shock.

"How could you kill him?" I sob.

"I had no more use for him. He was pretty useless anyway." He says with a shrug.

"You really don't care do you? At least Raphael has feelings once again. That's the difference between you two. He *wants* to change. He has something in his world that gives it meaning," I say.

"Enough!" he yells, causing me to jump. "Now it comes down to the crunch. I will offer you one lifeline because I'm feeling somewhat generous, even if you have thoroughly pissed me off and wasted my time. Just one chance though, I don't want you thinking I'm going soft, and believe me, there is *nothing* about me that is *soft*. Whatever you decide, you will not be leaving this building alive" he says. My heart falls into my stomach as I look into the eyes of death. "I should be killing you only. It was massively emphasized that you must croak it, kick the bucket, pop your clogs; however, you want to say it, but you are meant to meet a very definitive end. For a little fun, I will offer you a choice. Consider yourself incredibly lucky. I offer you immortality. I can turn you into one of my kind. It will terribly piss the others off and I will never hear the end of it, but there's nothing they will be able to do. I am sure Raphael will be so happy he will have a wet daydream. So, do you want me to turn you into a vampire? It will be excruciating of course, but my blood is so old it will be very quick. Have a really good think about it."

I sit and stare at him. THIS is his lifeline? THIS is what he thinks is a great option?

"Why would you offer me that if all you wanted to do was get rid of me?" I ask.

"Think about it, if you become a vampire you would no longer be in danger, you would also no longer be a liability to vampires."

"But that doesn't stop you from wanting me gone." I say with confusion

"That is true, but you have no idea how much of a reaction 'rocking the boat' will get. That would be far more entertaining, and it would last *forever*." He grins.

"You're actually serious aren't you?!"

"As serious as one can be," he says with a snide smile.

"But you'll get into so much trouble with The Synod because I'd be able to tell them you changed me." I say with raised eyebrows.

"Silly, silly girl. The only one who would believe you would be Raphael. The others would think you made it up to protect Raphael, the one they'd think who really changed you. Add to that the fact that Mathias will never think a bad thing about me because I am his vampire *son*." He says with quotation finger movements. He is beyond insane! How can he possibly think that he could get away with something like this? I most certainly don't want to be a vampire and in all honesty, I don't trust his word whatsoever.

"There is no way on this Earth that I would become a vampire! I'd rather die and rot!" I yell. My time on this Earth has been a short one, but I have known the joy of love, and if the afterlife exists. I will never forget that love!

"Alas, what a shame. It would have given me a laugh for many years to come, but it really doesn't make any difference to me," he admits. "Harry, you have a new task."

"What is it Reggie?" he asks.

"Drop Rosannah's dead body off on Raphael's doorstep," he says. I scream as Reggie lunges at me.

CHAPTER FIVE

Raphael

"Mathias, are you absolutely sure you know nothing of this?" I ask him. Nicholas has been crossed off the suspect list and the next in line is Reggie. He's the only other one who would even dream of taking Rosannah, but like usual, I have hit a brick wall.

"I've already told you, I know nothing and I know how you feel about Reggie, but he's been loyal to me. I've known him for over a thousand years. He's never betrayed me or any other vampire that I know of. It must be down to vampires outside of The Synod," he says. I know that it will take much more than my concerns to convince him, but still I try.

"How would vampires outside of The Synod and my family know about Rosannah? That does not make any sense unless one of us has told outsiders. Has it not even occurred to you that Reggie could be doing things behind your back?" I ask him.

"And could it not occur to you that anyone of your family members could have told other vampires?" He asks. Fury races through me and an uncontrollable growl escapes me.

"How dare you!" I yell at him.

"Now you know how I feel when you constantly accuse Reggie of things, especially something like this!" It does not do much to calm me down. "Look Raphael, you know as well as I do that there are a lot of vampires out there who are not too happy with you. It could be a number of them, and you also know as well as I do that any vampires out there could have overheard any our conversations," he says. That is a valid point, but my gut is still twisted with anger at his accusation. I do not have time for this. This is not about who does and does not know about Rosannah, it's about finding her as soon as possible before God knows what happens to her.

"What on Earth would you have me do? I *must* find her," I plead.

"I have no ..." *Ring*. My phone cuts him off.

"What is it?" I answer the phone without seeing who is calling. A lot of high pitched mumbles come down the line and I know it can only be my sister. "Evangeline, calm down and tell me slowly. I cannot understand a word you are saying." I say as soothingly as I can.

"It's Rosannah. She's here," she sobs. Her tone fills with me dread, not confidence.

"Is she okay?" I ask. A loud wail sounds down the line.

"She's dead!" She cries. I turn to Mathias who looks very grave.

"Are you sure?" I ask, because I don't want to believe her. This cannot be true. There *must* be a mistake. My sister is one of the most unintelligent creatures on Earth, she must have this wrong.

"Raphael! She's really dead!" she wails. I end the phone call and speed home without saying a word to Mathias. He's by my side when I arrive. I can hear Evangeline sobbing upstairs from the room that Rosannah had when she was here. I know my sister; she is having one her dumb moments. Somehow she thinks Rosannah's dead. I'm sure in five minutes we will all be laughing over how silly she has been.

"I'll call the twins and get them over here," Mathias says gravely and pulls out his phone.

"I am sure Evangeline is mistaken," I say as I race up to Rosannah's room.

I enter the room and my eyes quickly search it. There on the bed lies Rosannah. Evangeline is crouched on the floor, holding her hand and sobbing into it. "She's okay Evangeline, let me check her and you'll see," I breathe. Evangeline looks at me, her face filled with disbelief, but sure enough she moves out of the way. I walk over to Rosannah, she looks so peaceful and serene. She must be resting. Relief floods through me until I notice that things are amiss. The rosiness that normally graces her cheeks is gone, the warm tone and depth to her creamy skin is no longer evident and in its place is a dull, lifeless bluish grey. Her once pink lips are now blue and flat. Her chest and heart are still and ... quiet. For a moment I stand dumbfounded, saying nothing, feeling nothing, while my mind pieces everything together. Then the realisation hits me. The pain is sudden. Every single part of me is on fire and it's excruciating. I never knew pain like this existed.

I fall to my knees as my legs buckle beneath me. "AHHHHHHHHHHH!" I scream at the top of my lungs with as much force as I can muster. "Ahhh," I whimper as my strength abandons me. I do not know how long I am like this for, but it feels like forever as I stare at the lifeless body of my beloved.

"Raph," Lawrence coos. It is then I see that my brothers are either side of me, holding onto my arms, keeping me upright while I kneel on the floor, but I am beyond support. I am so broken and I will never mend.

I jump to my feet suddenly, jarring everyone around me.

"I want everyone out," I say.

"But Raphael," Mathias starts.

"GET OUT!" I yell. "Do not touch her. Leave her where she is and do not follow me. I wish to be left alone ... for eternity," I cry. I don't wait to see if they leave before running off to the crypt.

"She's no more," I sob as I flop on to my mother's coffin. "She has gone to where you are. Mother, how do I exist without her?" I ask. "I cannot even join you both!" I yell as sobs wrack through me and I cry like I have never cried before.

CHAPTER SIX

Rosannah

I think one of life's biggest mysteries is how it ends. Some of us think we know what death is all about, what it feels like, where we go to once we have passed on, but only those who have died really know what it's like. There are those out there who have experimented with death, like trying to bring the dead back to life but there are others who think that death and corpses should be left well alone. What about those who believe that death is an entity that follows us around? I don't know about any of that, but I have to admit, I have always been curious. Don't get me wrong, I have always loved living and I wasn't planning on finding out anytime soon, but I have always wondered what dying would be like, I couldn't help it. Maybe that's morbid, maybe that's weird, maybe it's actually normal, but either way, it never stopped me from questioning it. What would it feel like? Where would I go? Who would I see? Would it hurt?

Pain was my biggest concern, but now I know the answers to some of my questions. Did it hurt? No, not at all. Other ways of meeting your end perhaps *are* more painful, but you can only ever truly die once in this life, so even if I *did* ever want to experience a painful death, which I wouldn't, I couldn't. Where am I now? I honestly have no idea. Wherever it is, it's dark here. There's nothing but an enveloping blackness. There are no feelings, sensations, or light.

There are no emotions, and there's no one else here. There are only my thoughts. I could be an entity floating around for all I know. I have no idea how long I've been here, it's like time has stood still, but I do know one thing; I was somewhere with someone before. I can't remember who or where, but there was *someone*, that I am sure of. Then there was nothing.

I've been here, wondering around in *nothing* for *ages*. Wait, what's that? I hear something. A low rumble from afar that is steadily getting closer. I can't discern what it is yet. It could be ... oh no, what is that? It *tingles*, no it *hurts!* Oh fucking hell it hurts! The pain is fast, it is sharp, it is hard and unrelenting. The pain is everywhere. It runs through me, it's all around me. I am consumed by it but surrounded by it at the same time. I try to scream many times as the pain rages, but I can't. I try to give up, to sink to the bottom of the darkness and disappear into non-existence, but I can't even do that because I'm already dead. How do you let go if you've already passed on?

Eventually, the pain subsides enough for it to border on bearable and I hear voices echo around me. What the hell did I just experience? Did I travel through the gates of hell? Why on Earth would I be going to Hell? What have I done that would wind me up there? If I am in Hell I bet my mother has had something to do with it! My pain eases up some more and slowly morphs into pins and needles. I begin to feel my limbs once again. Suddenly the black turns into a blurry view. Did some evil minion of Satan just pull my eyelids open? The bastard! Why can't I rest in peace?

My vision slowly clears, and I realise that what I'm seeing is white and *very* textured. I look around and see a hanging light fitting. I'm looking at a ceiling! Oh. Ohhhhh. What ceiling looks like this? I go to move, but I'm up before I've really put much effort in it. Evangeline is in front of me. Why is Evangeline in Hell? Has the devil tried her image on for size?

"She's alive!" She squeaks. It *is* Evangeline. Surely the devil wouldn't go as far as to even squeak like her?

"Evangeline you idiot, she's not *really* alive!" I hear Lawrence yell. He appears in front of me. "This is incredible, how the hell did this happen?" Lawrence asks Nicholas joins him.

"She looks pretty freaked out," he says.

"Think about what she's been through," Lawrence whispers very quietly to him. I look at him. "Rosannah, did you hear that?" Lawrence asks. I nod my head.

"I have to tell Raphael," he says and dashes off. I watch him go. It's pretty weird, I can track his speed and I can see every movement. He's not slowed down at all. Wait, Raphael? I had forgotten about him. I'd forgotten about everyone. I look up at Nicholas and he's grinning from ear to ear. I'm not dead. No, I'm much worse than dead, I'm a vampire!

CHAPTER SEVEN

Raphael

My sobs are interrupted by loud footsteps.

"Raph, Raph!" Lawrence yells. There is an urgency and excitement to his words. I look up as he stops right next to me.

"There is no justification as to why you are here, go away!" I spit at him.

"Raph, she's not dead," he says.

"What?!" I yell. "She is dead! I saw her with my very own eyes. I know a dead body when I see one!" I yell. The words hit me once again and I double over in pain.

"No Raph, you don't understand. She's not dead, she's a vampire."

"What? What did you just say?" I ask as I look up at him.

"Rosannah, is a vampire," he says with a huge grin on his face. The joy that fills my chest is stifling. I cannot speak, I am bursting with happiness. I race to Rosannah's room without saying a word to Lawrence. I enter the room to see Rosannah standing in the middle of the room with Evangeline and Nicholas standing nearby.

"Rosannah you're...." My voice catches in my throat. She is beyond anything I have ever seen. I did not think it was possible for her to be more beautiful than she was, but I was so very wrong. Her beauty is exquisite and it is endless. Her light grey eyes connect with mine. I see a deep sadness, but it vanishes when she sees me. She moves at me with speed and hugs me. I can feel her strength as she holds me tight. It's a strange but very welcoming sensation coming from her.

"Raphael," she says with relief. I honestly thought I had lost her. I'm beyond ecstatic Rosannah is not dead, but Rosannah, a vampire? This is like a dream come true for me. I know it's selfish but I haven't wanted anything more than to have Rosannah forever. Now she is safe from harm and will never die from old age, disease or injury. "That monster did this to me," she says with a sob. I pull her back from me. As happy as I am, I cannot overlook the fact that a vampire has made Rosannah suffer.

"Who?" I ask.

"Reggie," she whispers. It may sound terrible, but I am not as mad as I should be. I am so happy that I still have my immortal Rosannah. However, don't get me wrong, I'm still enraged at Reggie. He *will* be punished, but my priority is Rosannah and getting her used to being like I am. I look around and see that Mathias is no longer here.

"Where's Mathias?" I ask.

"Well, you did throw everyone out. He left, we on the other hand ignored you," Nicholas says with a grin.

"Nothing new there then," I sigh.

"Raph, are you going to tell Mathias about Reggie?" Evangeline asks with her head cocked to the side.

"Telling Mathias can wait."

"Okay," she says. What? No argument? I give her a questioning look and she gives me an understanding look. If only she could always be like this. I'm sure she will make up for it soon enough.

"Let's all go and leave these two alone for a bit," Nicholas says to the others and gives me a knowing look.

"But how can we go when Rosannah has just become a vampire?" Evangeline asks.

"Evangeline, you can spend some time with Rosannah later, but at first let's give Raph and Rosannah some... privacy," Nicholas says as he leads a frowning Evangeline out of the room. Lawrence follows and soon after, I hear the front door close. I pull Rosannah into a tight hug and kiss the top of her head.

"I honestly thought I had lost you." I whisper. She pulls back from me and kisses me hard. I am rock hard in an instant but I do not act upon it. Now is not the best time to try and seduce her even though I want to. Soon Rosannah puts a hand between us and rubs my erection, moaning lightly as her palm slides up and down over the zipper of my jeans. "Are you sure?" I ask as I pull back from her to look into her eyes.

"I am devastated that I'm a vampire, but I've never wanted to make love to you more than I want to right now," she says. Wrapping an arm around her waist I jump taking her with me. We land on the bed with her on her back and me crouching with my knees either side of her hips. The bed collapses beneath us without putting up any fight. We writhe on the broken mattress and I have no intention of stopping.

"I hope you're not too attached to this particular outfit," I say through gritted teeth and Rosannah shakes her head. I grab the neckline of her top and rip it straight down the middle. I pull the wrecked garment off of her and it gives way at the sleeves. I stare at her shoulders remembering when we first made love. I had caused burns from gripping her top too tight. Her skin now is an immaculate creamy white and her eyes are jet black.

One by one, I take off her shoes and with a flick of my wrist I remove her bra. I grab the waist band of her jeans and rip them apart. I then rip her panties off. With Rosannah completely naked I cannot get my clothes off quick enough and I am on top of her within seconds.

"Tonight I want you to fuck me like you've never fucked me before," she says.

"Oh, I have every intention of doing exactly that," I say as I slam into her. She moans and the extreme tightness of her super strong muscles grip me. I cry out in ecstasy. Pulling back, I slam into her once again causing us to jump up the destroyed bed.

"Ah," I moan. "I know what to do to keep you in place." I grip Rosannah's hips. Holding on with all my might I slam into her as hard as I can. It is only a matter of seconds before I feel her muscles clench deliciously as she comes with a scream, causing me to climax too. "I will have you coming like that on my cock all night," I say and continue to pound into her. My cock slides in and out and rips another groan from me. Rosannah's moans build, getting louder as I feel her muscles tighten up again.

"Oh God, I'm going to come!" she screams. Tonight, it is all about making her come on my cock as many times as I am capable of doing. Somehow, I manage to keep going, but it's not long before we are both emotionally spent.

CHAPTER EIGHT

Rosannah

Last night was amazing. I had no idea how much better sex would be when you're a vampire. My first full vampire sex I might add. I hadn't realised that Raphael had been holding back that much when I was a human. I hadn't given it any thought, but if I had, I probably would have realised. If he'd been able to put his full strength into it without breaking me, it would have heightened the sensations to an out of this world pleasure. There's one major problem with that though; the pleasure would have been un-comprehendible. There was no way I'd have been able to imagine how *good* it would feel or how hard I would come *every time*. I really did think Raphael had let go before, but that was nothing compared to last night! And the bed? In the early hours of the morning he moved us into his room and disposed of it. He said the twins would be all over it if they saw the broken bed, but he doesn't seem to have realized that they'll spot that it's missing.

Well, that was another first for me. I've never broken a bed before, unless you count that one time Brianna and I used my bed as a bouncy castle. My mother had popped out to get her usual facial, manicure and pedicure. It was the first time I had actually managed to convince my mother to leave me behind. I have no idea how I managed it, but I had really tried because I *hated* going anywhere with my mother, *especially* to any kind of salon. She was demanding and completely expectant about how she should be treated. It was utterly humiliating and I would try my best to apologise to the people as much as I could without my mother noticing. Add to the whole experience of being pulled about, it really was an all-round pain in the butt.

On this particular occasion Brianna and I were eleven years old and it was wholly irresponsible for my mother to leave us home alone, but she did. It didn't take long for Brianna and I to get bored after she had gone. I can't remember whose idea it was to jump on the bed, but we both thought it would be great fun. We had a competition as to who could jump the highest. With us both being competitive as anything, it wasn't long before the bed broke.

When my mother returned she wasn't happy. Was she cross that we had broken the bed? Not exactly. She was mad because I had missed out on our *mother and daughter time* to play *who can jump the highest*. She apparently hadn't been able to enjoy her pampering session because I didn't want to go, but she did tell me that she would have been less disappointed if I'd have gone through her makeup bag and closet and wrecked all of her uber-expensive make up and clothes to play dress up. Another memory that still haunts me.

I remember when Brianna told her mother that mine had left us home alone, she hit the roof, but some spa treatment vouchers and goodies soon sorted that out. My mother has always been good at paying people off.

Silly memories like that are now a part of my old *life*. A life that is no longer mine. Everything is now unsettlingly different. This morning is my first as a vampire and I have the fastest shower I've ever had! I got dried and dressed in seconds. I'm now in the kitchen as it's breakfast time, but I know I won't be having food. It's just the routine I'm used to. Now I will have to have blood. The thought of drinking it puts a bad taste in my mouth. Vile, but at the same time I'm strangely curious. I know it's grasping at straws, but I'm trying to focus on the practicalities instead of all the things I can no longer do. One feeling that is familiar is that I'm hungry. However, it's not a normal hunger. It doesn't sit in my stomach, but instead at the back of my mind. It's lurking there in the background. It's hard to describe, but it's a bit like when you're not *actually* hungry but you feel like you should be eating something. There's no growling tummy, there's no pangs of hunger. No feeling parched or need of nourishment. I feel like I'm always sated, but could take a few bites of something if I fancied.

Raphael comes into the kitchen and pulls me from my thoughts. I watch as he makes his way to the fridge. Soon he joins me at the breakfast bar with a bottle of blood and a glass.

"The twins wanted to be present for this but I would not allow it," he admits as he pours the blood into the glass. I'm incredibly grateful they're not here. I could really do without their ridiculing at the moment. As the blood fills the glass the colour grabs my attention. I've seen blood before. I knew it wasn't always a good thing to see, but right now it has a twisted beauty to it. Like an enchanting liquid crystal, it glints and shines. It reflects the light spectacularly as it splashes its way into the glass tumbler. I watch the tiny bubbles as they form and rise to the top of the liquid. It completely captivates me. Raphael replaces the bottle on the bar and looks to me pulling my attention to him.

"How do you feel when you see this?" He asks me.

"Conflicted." I say looking back to the glass.

"How so?"

"The thought of drinking it grosses me out, but at the same time I find it appealing."

"It is human nature to be disgusted by this, but is not vampire nature. It really is mind over matter," he says and pushes the glass over to me. I pick it up and sniff it. It has a metallic smell that I used to hate, but now it smells incredible. That thought alone throws my mind into overdrive. It tells me that it's wrong to want to drink it yet at the same time tells me to drink it. I can't make up my mind if I should drink it or not so I slam the glass down and look at Raphael.

"This is very wrong; I shouldn't find this as appetising as I do. Can't I just eat food and force it down?" I ask with panic. Raphael's expression flashes with concern but he soon smooths his features.

"Rosannah, it is up to you if you decide to eat food, but you have to understand that your stomach will not be able to digest it and your body will reject it. Yes, you can use force to keep it in your stomach, but it will rot and you will be a calling card for flies and the like." I hold back a gag at the thought.

"So the choice I have is either blood, which I find hard to get my head around, or food that will rot in my stomach if I don't allow my body to throw it up?"

"Yes, essentially."

"What happens if I eat nothing?" I ask. Raphael lets out concerned sigh.

"Nothing will happen."

"That's ridiculous! What's the point in drinking blood if it doesn't sustain you?" I ask.

"Humans cannot be sustained on thrill seeking can they? No, they do it for pleasure."

"So vampires drink blood simply because they enjoy it?"

"Yes."

"How can you be certain I won't die? What's the longest a vampire has gone without blood that you know of?"

"For me, personally, I have gone seven months without blood, but I am also aware of a vampire who went seven hundred years without it. I can tell you with absolute certainty that they did not die." He says.

"So why did they start drinking it again?"

"They came to their senses. You are what you are and nothing can change that," he says with frustration.

"I was human and now I'm not. That was quite a change!"

"You did not have any part in that. It was forced upon you and now you cannot go back. Your body has changed too much to be reversed. Now, I will sit here with you for as long as it takes for you to take the first sip. The first sip is always the hardest, it is the mind that plays the blockade."

I pick up the glass with a huff and stare into it. Everything in my conscious mind is screaming at me not drink this stuff. This was pumping around a person's body recently. A living, breathing person whose heart is beating. I hesitate and go to put the glass back down.

"Right, rotten food it is then," Raphael says as he gets up.

"Oh for goodness sake!" I yell as I take a huge swig of the liquid. It's cold and thicker than water but not as thick as I thought it would be. It goes down smoothly and tastes metallic. Surprisingly, it tastes better than anything I have tasted before. I finish the glass and put it down. We sit in silence for some time staring at the empty tumbler until Raphael speaks.

"Was it as bad as you thought it would be?" Raphael asks.

"No. It was ... actually pretty tasty." I smile. Raphael laughs. "What? Have I got a blood moustache?" I ask, feeling self-conscious.

"No, your teeth are red." He laughs.

"How do I get rid of it!?" I ask with slight panic.

"Run your tongue over them with a swirl of saliva. Your strength will clean them." I feel doubtful about his suggestion but I give it a go.

"Has it worked?" I ask while smiling wide.

"Yes." I do believe him but I don't feel like that was enough to clean them

"Oh, I should clean my teeth too" I say getting up.

"With your ability to clean your own teeth it is not necessary, but it is entirely up to you."

"Do you still do it?" I ask.

"Yes, I do, "he says with a smile. Well that makes up my mind for me. I dash upstairs at speed and clean my teeth within seconds.

CHAPTER NINE

Raphael

Although I know I should have spoken to Mathias about Regius, my priority has been Rosannah. I have been worried about how she would take to blood and being a vampire. I need to make sure she is okay and be there for her. She could still fold but while she appears to be alright I can now talk to Mathias.

I pull out my phone and call him. Mathias answers at the first ring.

"Raphael, I am so very sorry for your loss," he says.

"Rosannah is not dead," I tell him.

"I know this must be absolutely awful for you but Rosannah is gone."

"No, you do not understand.Mathias, she is a vampire." There is a moment of silence on the line before he speaks.

"I'm on my way over," he says and the line goes dead. Within minutes he arrives. I let him in and he stops in the hallway.

"Where is she?" He asks. Rosannah races down the stairs and joins us.

"I'm here," she proclaims with a smile. Mathias turns to me with a look of concern.

"Raphael, did you do this?"

"No, Mathias. I was with you explaining that Rosannah was missing when this happened. It would have been impossible!"

"I know that dear boy, but is it not possible you put Rosannah into transition and then perhaps came to see me with a story of her missing?" he asks. I let out a growl and Rosannah lays a hand on my arm to calm me.

"I have already told you, I did not change her," I say with forced calm.

"You must understand why I would suspect you. Is it possible you got a vampire to do this for you?" He asks me.

"Certainly not! If it were my choice it would have been my blood that changed her, not another's," I say.

"If this was nothing to do with you who then?" He asks me.

"Why not ask Rosannah herself? She is standing right here." I signal to her.

"Oh, of course," he mumbles to himself as he turns to her.

"Who is responsible for this?" He asks her.

"Reggie is," she says with conviction. Mathias frowns.

"What happened?" He asks her.

"Reggie has been behind the whole entire thing. He brainwashed Alex to pursue me numerous times and when that didn't work he sent a vampire, Harry, to kidnap me. Killing me was part of his plan, but he offered me the chance to become one of you. I declined but he turned me anyway." Knowing she has suffered at the hands of Regius stabs at my chest. The vermin even had the nerve to change Harry. The fact that he is now a vampire disgusts me.

"Rosannah, maybe your transition has been a bumpy one, but there is no way on this Earth that

Reggie would do any such thing," he says. I am uncertain of how I look, but it has plastered fear on Rosannah and Mathias's faces. I stalk towards Mathias as rage flows through me.

"Are you telling Rosannah that she is lying?" I ask through gritted teeth. Mathias backs up until he hits the wall.

"Raphael calm down," Rosannah pleads. I am utterly furious but I must keep myself in check. I am capable of killing Mathias and he, Rosannah, and I know it.

"I'm not saying she is lying, but perhaps mistaken. There's no way Harry is a vampire. No one would change him," he says thoughtfully "It's also hard to believe that Reggie is behind all of this. It goes against what he stands for and it goes against me. He is in all purposes, my son. I made him," he says with a sad look in his eyes.

"Reggie said he'd get away with it because he did not think you'd believe me. He's fully reliant on it." Rosannah says with worry.

"It is time to wake up and see things for what they truly are. Transitions are turbulent, heck they are a damn monsoon, tornado and earthquake all rolled into one but it should not cloud judgement. If Rosannah says it was Regius who did, this then it was Regius." I say.

"You've had it in for Reggie from the very first time you met him. It appears that it affects *your* ability to see things for what they are," he says. Rage fills me again. I punch my fist into the wall right next to his head causing both him and Rosannah to yelp in surprise.

"No Mathias, it is your fatherly love that is the problem with judgement. I suggest you leave before I do something that I may regret," I threaten. Mathias looks a little shocked but he holds his head high as he leaves. Once the front door closes Rosannah speaks.

"I can't believe he doesn't believe me. Reggie was right."

"I will make Mathias understand, but for now I will give him a little time. The news is too difficult a mouthful for him to swallow. Right now there are much more important things to worry about," I say taking Rosannah in my arms.

"Like what?" She asks with a naughty sparkle to her eyes.

"Like helping you get to grips with your new strength and abilities." A look of disappointment befalls her features. She has much to learn and this is start tomorrow. "Do not worry, there is plenty of time for anything else you may want to do." I smile and take her mouth with mine.

CHAPTER TEN

Rosannah

While Raphael sleeps I lay awake in his bed staring at the ceiling after a marathon night of making love. That's two nights in a row. I could get used to this. Could this be my forever? Making love every night with Raphael, spending infinity with him? Could our love last that long? I definitely hope so, but what about marriage? I know that vampires get married but does that mean I ever will? I don't see Raphael as the type who wants to get married. And what about kids? I know I'll never be able to have kids. I can't imagine Raphael as a dad. Pain pangs at me and I have to get up and do something to take my mind off of it. I look at the clock, it's 5:35am. I get up and have a shower.

By the time I've finished Raphael is awake. He smiles nervously at me before heading into the shower himself. I wait for him so we can have breakfast blood together. He comes down and sorts out the blood for us without saying a word and we end up drinking it in silence. I can tell that something is going on and all sorts of worries fill my mind. Raphael pulls me from my thoughts by getting his phone out and calling Evangeline.

"I need you here to help Rosannah take the jump," he says and hangs up. The jump? What the hell? Within minutes she's here and smiling away at me. Oh, so she knows what's going on. Raphael then phones Lawrence.

"I do not want you or Nicholas here today, do you understand?"

"Are you doing the jump?" asks Lawrence. I can hear him as clear as day and Raphael looks at me knowingly.

"That is none of your concern," he says.

"Oh come on Raph, we have *got* to see this," says Lawrence.

"Categorically not. You will just be a hindrance," he says and hangs up. I love Raphael dearly but sometimes his people skills are much to be desired. "Let us head outside."

I follow him and Evangeline out onto the veranda. Raphael's face turns into a scowl when he sees the twins waiting on the grass for us. Even though everything appears to be okay, I still feel slightly funny around Nicholas. I find it a little difficult to trust him completely. I'm about ninety-nine point nine percent there, but the remaining nought point one percent is still apprehensive.

"I told you two not to be here!" Raphael yells.

"And miss Rosannah's big day? Not a chance," says Lawrence. Big day? I really don't like the sound of this. Raphael growls at him but turns to Evangeline.

"Evangeline, could you please check the parameters just to make sure we are not seen?" He asks and she takes off. What wouldn't he want seen? It only takes minutes before Evangeline returns.

"All clear," she grins.

"All of you except Rosannah will know why we are here," Raphael says. The twins snicker but a glare from Raphael cuts them off. So they all know what this is all about and not me? Great. Raphael turns to me with a concerned smile. "You are going to do some jumping. Whether you are aware of it or not, you have incredible strength. It will be hard for you to comprehend just how strong you are. How do you think it is possible you can move at the speed you do? It is down to your strength as well as agility. Once you have an idea of those, it should not be too hard for you to control them and use them in a way you find useful."

"I don't feel that strong," I say. It's my honest opinion. I don't feel weak at all, but I don't feel power coursing through me, I don't feel coiled up like I'm ready to spring.

"You are strong enough to jump over a five storey building and clear it," he says. I stare at him like he's sprouted an extra head.

"How the hell do you expect me to jump that high?!" I exclaim.

"I do not," he says. "I expect you to jump over that," he says pointing to the wall at the very bottom of the garden.

"You must be joking!" I tell him. A frown appears on his face as the twins laugh. Evangeline scowls at them.

"Rosannah, the wall is only two meters high," he says as if it's nothing. "We will show you how to jump over it after I talk you through it." He says as he places his hand at the small of my back. "You could do this from a walking pace but I would suggest for your own peace of mind that you run. You do not need to run at full speed. You currently have no knowledge of how to time your jump if you run at full speed. Once you are roughly five meters away from the wall you will need to jump if you run at a human pace. The kind of pace you used when you ran from me." The Twins burst out laughing.

"You kept that one to yourself," says Nicholas.

"Yeah, anyone would think he didn't want his dear brother to know," laughs Lawrence. Raphael ignores them and continues.

"Bend your knees and push down through your toes like this," he says as he signals to Evangeline. She bends her knees and jumps twice my height and lands gracefully back on the ground. "The momentum you have created with your running should take you forward. You will also want to land on bended knees, just as Evangeline has showed you."

"Why would I want to land like that? I thought I was supposed to be *indestructible*."

"You are; it is just a smoother landing. Although it does not hurt either way, it is not very pleasant and is quite jolting. Now we will all show you how it is done," he says.

I watch as they all take it in turns to run and jump over the wall each way. They make it look so incredibly easy and graceful and once they are done, they are back with me. Oh great, the twins have started doing their hand signals.

"I don't even want to know what outcomes you are betting on," I admit.

"You really don't." Nicholas laughs.

"Go when you are ready. The most important thing to remember is that you cannot hurt yourself," Raphael says, ignoring the twins.

"Unless you include your pride," jokes Lawrence. Raphael growls at him and I faze them all out of my mind as I mentally prepare myself. I may be indestructible but I don't feel like it. I mean, I can whizz around at some speed. I feel light and somewhat clear inside of my mind and body. I feel fully refreshed. It's incredible, you have no idea how many little aches and pains you have until they are gone. I suck in a huge breath, out of nervousness from habit and start running. As I make my way to the wall I remember back to when I ran in an attempt to get away from Raphael. That was when he had shown me the garden when I was first held captive here and he had let his guard down as we passed the entry gate. I took the opportunity to run as fast as I could to his next door neighbour's bungalow. That's the kind of speed Raphael wants me to run at. Thankfully, I didn't ring the doorbell, but I remember my legs tiring, my lungs stinging, and my body struggling. There's none of that now. I feel like I could run like this forever, but there's still that little human voice inside my head that's telling me the tiredness will come.

"You can do it," yells Evangeline from far behind me. I think she's right. I can do this; I am full of energy. I'm sure I can do this. Right, I'm five meters from the wall, jump. No! The wall is too big! Abort mission, I repeat abort mission!

"She's chickening out!" Lawrence laughs. Bastard!

I try to stop but I'm too late. I put my hands up to protect my face as I collide with the wall with a deafening crash. I feel little tremors around me as debris hit the ground around me. Once I've skidded to a holt I keep my eyes clenched tight. I'm meant to be indestructible but how the hell do I know that for sure? What if my transition cocked up somehow and I still have human traits? Right now I could have broken bones sticking out of my torn and bloodied flesh, numbed by a gazillion tons of adrenaline pumping through my supposed redundant veins! I wait for the pain, not knowing what damage I've done and where I've ended up.

"Rosannah, are you okay?" Raphael asks right by my ear.

"Raph, of course she's okay. She's a vampire!" Says Evangeline.

"I am fully aware of that. I am checking if she is *feeling* okay," Raphael grates at her. I can't help but laugh.

"Why are you laughing? You should see what you've done." Nicholas laughs. Slowly I open my eyes and look at Raphael. He gives me a soft smile.

"I think I'm okay."

"*You* might be alright but the wall isn't." Lawrence laughs. I turn and see that there's a huge gap in the wall and broken bricks and debris is scattered all around us.

"I did *that*?" I ask incredulously.

"When a vampire plays chicken with anything the vampire always wins. This time the losing party was Raphael's wall," says Nicholas.

"I thought that I was meant to be able to jump over that bloody thing!" I say.

"That would involve actual jumping, something you left out." Lawrence laughs. His sarcasm rubs me up the wrong way.

"Oh right, so if that's true I should be able to just jump over that bit over there!" I say angrily pointing to a part of wall that has been left unscathed.

"Of course," chirps Evangeline.

"Fine!" I exclaim. I run over to the wall and jump. The air turns cold as I whizz through it. It causes my hair to whip at my face. Everything below me shrinks away almost instantly. My arms and legs flail as I become completely weightless. As soon as I take in just how high I am I start to fall at an alarming rate.

"Geronimo!" Shouts Lawrence.

"Oh shit! She's going to crater, everyone move back!" Yells Nicholas. I brace myself for the landing expecting it to be hard but instead it's soft and gives way. I end up stuck up to my waist in mud with a large crater around me.

"Why did you do that?" Asks a confused Evangeline who appears at the edge of the crater. The twins appear but soon vanish. I can hear them laughing their heads off! Raphael jumps down in to the crater and pulls me out.

"Why did you do that?" He asks softly in my ear.

"Believe it or not, I was a little dubious about having the ability to jump like a human sized grasshopper," I answer.

"Well now you know. It is best if you go and get cleaned up," he says with a warm and knowing smile. I sigh and walk past the twins who are still laughing, rolling around on the floor.

CHAPTER ELEVEN

Raphael

While Rosannah is having a shower and getting cleaned up I sit at the breakfast bar with Evangeline and a glass of blood.

"Don't worry Raph, I'm sure she's fine. At least she knows her own strength now." She smiles. She *is* right. Sometimes Evangeline manages to talk sense. It is a rare occurrence, but it does happen from time to time. I can hear the twins before they enter.

"You are not wanted here, go away," I say with distain.

"Such a funny way our brother has to show us how much he truly loves us," says Lawrence.

"Yeah, I can really feel that love," replies Nicholas.

"You know, you two did not help Rosannah out in the slightest," I tell them.

"Oh come on, it was hilarious, admit it." Lawrence laughs.

"I did not find it funny in the slightest. Have you forgotten what she is going through? The things she has to deal with? The things she has lost?" I ask.

"My transition isn't something I spent a lot of time thinking about to be honest. I got over it a long time ago. You've got to learn to laugh Raph and pull out that stick that's so firmly stuck up your ass." He laughs. "Anyway, I'm heading off now that the show is over, see you later," says Lawrence as he disappears out of the front door.

"I better go to." Evangeline smiles and follows, leaving just Nicholas and myself. Nicholas and I have not had a decent talk since before he ran off after the fight we had about Rosannah. The silence does not take long until it becomes uncomfortable.

"Nicholas, do you have something you would like to discuss with me?" I ask as I turn to face him. He clears his throat and jerkily nods.

"I, I need some advice," he says and my eyebrows shoot up.

"I am not too sure how I can be of assistance but I will listen," I tell him. It looks as if Nicholas has forgotten everything because why else would he be seeking my advice over Lawrence's. A dark thought occurs to me.

"I will only tell you this once, if this is a part of any crazy plan that includes Rosannah I will personally see to it that your existence is a misery," I warn. Nicholas looks shocked but shakes his head.

"No, it's nothing to do with Rosannah," he says.

"Very well, go ahead," I tell him.

"I'm sure that you know I have a relationship with Brianna," he starts. I raise a questioning eyebrow but Nicholas continues. "I know that our relationship started off shaky,"

"Huh," I interrupt him. It is very uncharacteristic of me, but it was uncontrollable. Nicholas's eyes narrow at me but he continues.

"Anyway, I've grown to like her, I mean really, really like her,"

"Do you love her?" I ask him, interrupting again.

"God, you are the worst for asking advice from. You keep interrupting," he says with frustration.

"I am so very sorry that I find any of what you have said surprising," I say deadpan.

"That makes sense now, but not for the other times you've interrupted me while I've been asking for advice!" he complains.

"Just get on with it," I demand.

"What I'm trying to say is that I want to tell Brianna the truth," he says with a sigh.

"I do not think she will enjoy hearing about how you went crazy over Rosannah," I say.

"I'm not talking about Rosannah!" he yells.

"How do you expect your relationship to last if you keep secrets from her?" I ask him.

"I will at some point but you're one to talk! I don't suppose you've told Rosannah how she happened to *really* come to evaluate your house? Or what you had originally intended to do to her?" he asks. I sit there quiet for a small while. He is right of course, but I do not want to fully admit that.

"I was somewhat distracted by the fact that Rosannah was kidnapped and then thinking she was dead. Do forgive me," I tell him sarcastically.

"That's a good enough reason ... for now, but that doesn't explain why you didn't tell her before," he says. Again, he has a point but I will not admit that.

"We are not discussing my relationship with Rosannah, but yours with Brianna."

"What a cop out," he says. A glare from me gets the message across.

"I want to tell Brianna about me being a vampire. I like her so much that I feel the time has come to tell her the truth. Depending on how well she takes it then

I will tell her about Rosannah and everything else," he says.

"Ah, I see. What advice is it you are actually after?"

"I'm not sure if it's a good idea," he says with concern.

"I think it is a great idea. You should do it. If she does not react well to your revelations then you can simply brainwash her to forget," I say with a smile.

"I know I can, but then why am I so nervous about it?" he asks me. The answer is very clear and another surprise to me.

"Because dear brother, you are in love with her," I say.

"I thought I was in love with Rosannah before, but it turned out I was so very wrong," he says with a frown. My shoulders tense but I roll them in a bid to relax them.

"I do not think you were ever in love with her," I say.

"I agree; I think I was just jealous but I don't understand why."

"I honestly do not know, but I can guess," I reply.

"And what is your guess?" he asks.

"You saw someone close to you find their soul mate. My guess is that you were jealous that you had not found yours, that someone else had what you did not," I say and place a hand on his shoulder.

"You know what, I think you're right. Now that I have these feelings for Brianna I'm no longer interested in Rosannah. I don't think I ever truly was. When I had that talk with her it was then that I realised just how foolish I had been. I'm so sorry brother!" he says and wraps his arms around me.

"It is okay; I do forgive you. There is just one more thing though," I say as he lets go of me.

"What's that?" he asks.

"I think you should discuss Brianna with Rosannah first," I say. A look of worry crosses Nicholas's face but it smooths out. Rosannah appears next to me.

"What about Brianna?" she asks looking and smelling clean and fresh.

"I want to tell her the truth about me and how our relationship started," he tells her.

"Well, you best make sure you don't hurt her mister!" she says as she stalks towards him, finger prodding his chest. Nicholas cowers from her and nods profusely. He then takes off out of the front door. I chuckle to myself. Rosannah really is a force to be reckoned with. That reminds me, I really must see Lawrence. I need to talk with him without Rosannah being able to overhear. Lawrence is the one I see for advice. It may sound farfetched, but Lawrence is very good at giving advice. It makes me wonder why Nicholas has ever come to me for it.

"Will you be okay while I head over to see Lawrence?" I ask Rosannah. Her eyebrows rise questioningly but she smiles at me.

"I need to visit home anyway. Poor Marmalade," she frowns.

"The neighbour has been feeding her for you. I saw to it," I say. Rosannah's face lights up. "I will see you later at your flat," I say with a smile and dash off to Lawrence's house.

Lawrence opens the door as I arrive.

"Hello brother, did you miss me?" He grins.

"Lawrence, there are some things I must discuss with you," I say, ignoring his question.

"Fire away," he says as he leans his back against the hallway wall.

"I am a little worried about Rosannah."

"Why? She's been doing so well. Add to that the fact she's immortal and indestructible, I'd say she's pretty more than okay,"

"That is where my worry lies. She is handling all of this *too* well. She would have preferred if she were dead than to be one of us, yet she is fine about all of this? Think back to when we were newly created vampires, the novelty wore off very quickly. Remember just how insane we all became before we accepted our fate?" I ask him. Lawrence lets out a belly laugh and I have to wait several minutes before he finishes. "How is this in any way funny to you?" I ask him through gritted teeth.

"This is Rosannah you're talking about. Give the girl more credit! She's so much stronger than we were. The woman takes *everything* in her stride. Think about the crap she had to put up with when she met you and all that followed. None of it has broken her, but only made her stronger. Do you not see just how funny it is that you are actually worried she can't handle being a vampire?" he says incredulously. I stare at him for a moment while I process what he has said.

"My God ... you are right. How could I ever doubt her?" I ask feeling a little ashamed.

"You love her and you're doing what comes with that. You worry about those you love," he replies. Do you see what I mean? Lawrence is surprisingly good at this kind of thing. Lawrence has a way of speaking sometimes, like he is speaking from experience. Especially when it comes to love. Lawrence has always denied that he has ever been in love, but I have my suspicions. If anyone would know it would be Nicholas, but he has denied that Lawrence has been in love too.

"You are right," I say with a relieved smile.

"Did you say there was more you wanted to discuss?" he asks.

"Oh, yes. I err, want to ask Rosannah to move in with me but I do not know if she would want to," I say. Lawrence's face lights up like a Christmas tree. He pushes himself off the wall, takes my hand, shakes it and pats me on the back.

"Who would have thought at three hundred years old you'd finally grow up," he says. I growl at him but he chuckles. "There's no way Rosannah would say no."

"You think?"

"You're kidding me right? Of course she'll say yes!"

"Even after I tell her how she came to evaluate my house?" I ask with concern.

"Even after that," he says and lets go of my hand.

"Please do me one small favour, don't tell Evangeline yet. I may be indestructible but I do fear that she will kill me through the screaming and squealing alone," I admit. Lawrence gives me a knowing look.

"Raph, it may be none of my business, but what the heck happened to Rosannah's bed? It seems to have disappeared," Lawrence asks. Lawrence misses nothing.

"You are right, it most certainly is none of your business," I say and run home to waste some time before I head to Rosannah's. I will be asking Rosannah to move in with me and I am nervous, something I am certainly not accustomed to. I am still amazed at how *human* Rosannah can make me feel.

CHAPTER TWELVE

Rosannah

I arrived home feeling a little guilty. I wanted to thank Brianna's mum for taking care of Marmalade, but I don't yet know how to do the eye colour thing. I will have to ask Raphael to show me how it's done when he arrives. I can't imagine Raphael with normal coloured eyes. I'm so used to his white, grey and black ones.

Marmalade danced around my ankles and I picked her up. I nuzzled my nose into her neck. I was surprised by how much I missed her.

"My beautiful girl, I've missed you so much." I cooed at her.

"Reow," she replied. After a while I placed her back down much to her dislike. I looked at the answer machine and moaned. It was full again. Why was I even surprised? I hit play and listened to all the messages. They generally asked where I was in varying degrees. I steadied myself, picked up the receiver and speed dialled my mother.

"Rosannah," she answered after one ring.

"Hello mother," I sighed.

"Oh, you want to call me that? You certainly don't treat me like it," she said.

"I've been really busy," I told her. I couldn't possibly have told her the truth, well, she wouldn't believe me anyway.

"Too busy to call your own mother? I didn't bring you up to be like this. How is that girlfriend of yours?" she asked.

"Mother! I do NOT have a girlfriend and you know it!" I yelled.

"Don't you raise your voice at me! It must be that girlfriend of yours, a terrible, terrible influence if you ask me."

"We've been through this before, I don't have a girlfriend, not that there is anything wrong with that," I told her deliberately, not apologising for yelling at her.

"Well, I know exactly why you have been busy," she said.

"Oh really? Go on then, tell me what you think it is this time,"

"I don't think Rosannah, I *know*. You're a drug dealer." I held back the biggest urge to laugh. "It's not the way I would have wanted you to make money but..."

"Mother, *please* stop there! I am not a lesbian and I am certainly not a drug dealer." I said trying not to laugh.

"I don't know what I did so wrong with you. I did everything possible to get you to follow in my footsteps. Look at Brianna, she has an incredibly good looking boyfriend. Looks stinking rich too, but you? No, you have to throw words around like *self* and *worth*." She said incredulously.

"You've met Michael?" I asked suspiciously.

"Yes. I came to your flat to see where you were. I was surprised to find that you hadn't been there for a while and that Brianna's mother was feeding *the cat*.

It was while I was talking to Nora that Brianna came to see her with Michael," She said. I didn't know what was more shocking. The fact that she met *Michael* or the fact that she had even bothered to come to my flat to see where I was. "That Michael really is something. If you had any sense you'd ask Brianna if he had a brother that she could set you up with," she said. Oh good God, could you believe it? I'd had enough!

"Mother, I have a boyfriend thank you very much and don't need you or Brianna to set me up with anyone," I said in a frustrated rush.

"Don't lie to me Rosannah, it's so beneath you." She chastised me.

"But it's actually true!" I said in exasperation.

"I suggest you dump that girlfriend of yours and focus on selling..." I hung up on her at that point. I didn't even want to think of what she was about to say to me. The phone rang straight away and I pulled the plug out.

Thirty minutes later I'm curled up on the couch with Marmalade watching one of the many music channels my digital box has. Thinking about my mother I know she really is a pain in the ass but in her own unique way she really does care about me. I keep telling myself that.

The front door opens and closes and Raphael is sat next to me puling me from my thoughts.

"You know, you don't disappear and reappear in a blur anymore," I say.

"That is because your eyes can see me move at my full speed," he says. "Is everything okay? You seem a little down?"

"I phoned my mother."

"Ah, I see."

"Can you believe that she thinks the reason I've not called is because she thinks I'm a drug dealer? She thinks I'm a lesbian too." I say.

"A lesbian?" he asks with confusion.

"Yep. She told me she had met Michael and suggested that if he has a brother, I should ask Brianna to set me up with him. How ironic is that?" I ask. Raphael pulls a face but I carry on. "I told her I have a boyfriend and she didn't believe me. She always wanted me to marry rich and divorce like she did. She was never happy that I had morals."

"We will have to sort this out once and for all. We should arrange for me to meet her."

"Are you sure you want to do that?" I ask. Raphael really doesn't know what he's letting himself in for.

"I will be honest. I do not particularly want to meet her. She sounds quite foul but I will do what I must to get the crazy ideas out of her head. Failing that myself, or you for that matter, can brainwash her."

"For you to meet her we'll have to sort out my eye colour. If my mother sees my eyes she'll completely freak out. She'll probably think I've gone blind from drug use! How do I make them normal?" I ask.

"You concentrate on them," he says simply. I turn my attention to my eyes and imagine them their normal colour. I can feel a kind of *shift* across my irises.

"Like this?" I ask dubiously.

"Yes." Raphael smiles.

"How do I get them to stay?" I ask.

"You can control the muscles of your irises too, just like any muscle in your body, so once they are their natural colour you can keep it there."

"What about when they are black? I know the black eyes are controlled by emotions, so would they override my natural colour if I was showing it?" I ask.

"That can be hard to control unless you have great control on your emotions," he says darkly.

"Raphael?" I ask.

"Yes?"

"Can you show me your eye colour?" I ask wanting to see what Raphael once looked like. I watch in amazement as dark brown and black bleed into the light grey. I gasp as I look into Raphael's chocolate brown eyes. Soon a flush tints his skin. "You look so wonderful and ... alive," I admit with amazement. I reach out and touch his face. His skin is still cold but he looks so human. I lean forward and kiss his now deep pink lips. It starts tenderly but soon Raphael's hands are at the small of my back massaging circles into my muscles. I groan and pull back. Raphael's brown eyes are now black and his tinted skin and lips are back to pale.

CHAPTER THIRTEEN

Rosannah

After pulling myself away from Raphael, I get out of bed and have a shower. Once I'm washed and dressed I sit with Marmalade and wait for Raphael to wake. I have no blood here so I can't have breakfast but I'm not really fussed.

It's not long before I hear light footsteps coming up the stairs towards my front door. There's no heartbeat accompanying them so I instantly know that whoever it is, they are a vampire. The bell rings and after placing Marmalade down gently I have the door open before they can ring the bell. It's Cindy and she looks incredibly upset but very confused.

"Rosannah, why don't you have a heartbeat anymore?" she asks.

"I, well, err. I'm a vampire now."

"So Raphael changed you?" she asks.

"No, it was against my will."

"Oh my goodness!" she exclaims.

"It's a long story. You look really upset, what's wrong?" I ask as I put an arm around her shoulder, push the door shut and guide her to the couch.

"It's Alex. A lady walking her dog found his dead body dumped on a hikers trail yesterday evening. He'd been there a little while and his neck had been so badly broken it was obliterated," she says through tearless sobs. Oh my God! I have been so wrapped up in being a vampire that I had forgotten all about Alex.

"Cindy, I'm so sorry. I know who killed him," I say feeling incredibly guilty that I hadn't said anything before.

"How do you know who killed him?" She asks in confusion.

"I was there," I admit quietly. "I am so sorry I didn't say anything before!"

"It's okay Rosannah, I know that you have just gone through something terrible," she says placing a hand on my shoulder. "What happened to Alex?" she asks.

"Vampires had wanted to get rid of me so they brainwashed Alex to get me several times but all their attempts failed. I was then kidnapped and Alex was killed."

"Who did this?" she asks.

"Reggie, and he turned Harry into a vampire. It was Harry who kidnapped me." I say.

"Someone should tell Mathias!" she says and stands.

"He already knows but he's having a hard time taking it in. We're giving him a little time to let the news sink in," I say and Cindy sits back down.

"Why would Reggie kidnap you?" she asks.

"The initial plan was to kill me because Reggie considered me a liability, but he turned me against my will instead," I say. Cindy's face lights up.

"You look incredible!" She exclaims but her smile fades. "It's just that Alex is dead" she sobs.

"I know, it's awful and it's all my fault," I say and pull her into a hug. Cindy pulls back and holds my shoulders.

"It most certainly isn't your fault and we'll sort this all out after the funeral. That's actually why I'm here.

I wanted to ask you if you'd come to Alex's funeral? It's being held in three days' time at mine and Vladimir's home. I know it's very soon but we want to lay him to rest as soon as possible. His mum is devastated," she says. She may have said that Alex's death isn't my fault, but I know if it wasn't for me and my inability to be brainwashed then Reggie, Harry, and whoever else they're working with wouldn't have felt the need to find a way to silence me. Although I'm pretty sure Reggie didn't need an excuse to ensure I wasn't able to say anything.

"Yes, I'll definitely be there," I say forcing a small smile.

"That's great. There's one more thing I wanted to ask before I go. I know how amazing you are at singing. Would you sing at Alex's funeral? I know the perfect song." She smiles at me. Karaoke is one thing but in front of grieving audience is another.

"Well, um, ah." I don't know what to say.

"You won't be singing alone, you will be singing with all of Alex's brothers," Cindy says encouragingly. Does that make it any easier? Cindy gives me a pleading look and I feel like I can't deny her.

"Okay, I'll do it," I say reluctantly.

"Oh Rosannah, you're awesome, you know that?!" she yells and pulls me into a tight hug. She lets go of me and pulls some paperwork out of her bag and hands it to me. "Here are the lyrics to the song and your parts are highlighted in pink. There's also all of Alex's brothers phone numbers. I'm sure you will need to practice with them at some point." She smiles. I take the paperwork and eye the song. It's one of my favourites. With eyes that have the inability to well up I look at her.

"The song is perfect," I say.

"It is, isn't it? Oh, could you tell Raphael he is welcome to come to Alex's funeral too," she says. We hear a quick shuffling sound coming from my bedroom and Raphael appears next to me in just his jeans. I watch as Cindy's eyes rake over his naked chest with appreciative eyes. Why the hell did Raphael not put a top on? I know Cindy is happy with Vladimir but watching her ogle at Raphael stirs something deep within me. She turns and gives me a knowing look. It's pretty obvious what we were doing last night.

"I am sorry for your loss. I am afraid I will not be able to attend because..." I give Raphael a glare that cuts him off. He looks slightly frightened but his face smooths back over.

"I will be happy to attend," he says with a light smile.

"Thank you Raphael," she says. "How are you finding vampire life?" she asks me.

"It's okay I guess," I say with a shrug. Would that be a blur to human eyes? I wonder.

"Okay? Rosannah has taken to being a vampire like a duck to water. Her ability to handle her transformation has been very admirable," Raphael exclaims.

"And she looks amazing too," Cindy adds.

"She certainly does," Raphael agrees.

"I best be off; I've got a lot of people to get around. The family is huge and Alex knew a lot of people," she says with sadness. "See you soon," she says and dashes out of the door. I frown as I hear Cindy leave out of the main door downstairs.

"What is wrong?" Raphael asks as he puts his arms around my waist. Her staring at your chest!

"I've got this song I now have to practice. I'm staying here for the day to get some practice in," I say, half lying.

"Oh my," Raphael says.

"What?" I ask.

"You are jealous," he says. I pull away from him.

"Well of course I am, she was openly ogling you," I say and cross my arms.

"You have no reason to be jealous."

"And you had no reason to come in here without your top on. You knew what you were doing. Now leave me to practice, you'll be too much of a distraction," I say trying not to laugh. Raphael gives me a cocky grin, dashes into my room, puts the rest of his clothes on and dashes out of my front door.

CHAPTER FOURTEEN
Raphael

That one day that Rosannah needed has extended. Although we have spoken on the phone several times, it has been three days since I last saw her. She has ploughed herself into learning this song, of which I have no idea what one it is. I have left her to practice, but I have to admit that Rosannah practicing the song with four other guys has not sat well with me. I have also decided to wait until after the funeral to ask her to move in with me. It makes sense to wait, vampires do not usually wait, but I do not want to upset Rosannah, I know she is sad about Alex's death.

After getting ready I head over to Rosannah's. I pull up outside of her apartment and she is in my car within seconds. I am surprised by just how much I have missed her. She is in a tight fitting black dress. I growl my approval and even though she smiles at me I can see a sadness in her eyes.

"It's crazy, but I've really missed you," she admits and leans forward, placing a light kiss on my lips. I smile at her knowingly. We pull away from the curb and head to Vladimir's house. "Work have left me lots of messages asking where I am. I don't know how to brainwash anyone," she admits with a sigh.

"I can sort them out for you if you would like. Just tell me what you want them to think. I can then show you how to do it at a time that is of your choosing."

"That'd be great. Just get them to believe that I've been on holiday."

We arrive at Vladimir's house quicker than last time. With Rosannah now a vampire I can really out my foot down. I normally speed when I am on my own or with other vampires. I generally know when I am safe to speed. With my vampire senses I know roughly where other vehicles and humans are so I am no danger to anyone or anything. I have been caught speeding a plethora of times by cameras, but a little brainwashing always gets me out of it. I visit my local council quite often, to sort out anything I do not like that goes on in the borough I live in, as well as sorting out my speeding tickets.

After I have parked I go to help Rosannah out of the car but she is already out when I get to her side.

"I'm capable of getting out myself you know." She laughs.

"I know, but I still want to be a gentleman." I take her hand and we head inside. The butler directs us to the same room that held Cindy's revealing party. The room is full of people sat in rows. They are muttering irrelevant chatter among themselves. Rosannah lets go of my hand and points to some seats that are empty near the front. I make my way there as she heads to a group of men. I can only assume they are Alex's brothers because they all look very similar to him. As I take a seat, I notice the closed casket at the top of the room. From what I have heard about Alex's death, it is probably better that he is not on display to the humans here.

There are lots of flowers around and two large pictures of Alex either side of the carved, dark wooded coffin. A clergy man walks in front of the casket and clears his throat. As he starts the service I zone out. I was once religious. When I was human it did not matter what walk of life you were from, you believed in God. People were shunned for all sorts of things back then, but if you did not believe in God you were worse than the devil himself as far as anyone was concerned. I stopped believing in God the day I became a vampire. That day changed a lot of things for me, but losing one's faith in something that I was so sure of was very unsettling. During our insane years my brothers, sister and I went on a search for God. It is safe to say that we never found God. I eventually got over it.

I do not know what the clergyman has said but Rosannah and Alex's brothers take to front of the room. Rosannah has been very secretive as to what song they are singing. She only told me that it is perfect.

The four brothers start humming in a quartet. The notes sound familiar but I still cannot place the song. After a lengthy introduction one of the brothers starts to sing. I know the song very well. Sobs start to ring out in the room as Rosannah starts to sing, "Caravan of Love" beautifully.

Cindy grabs the hand I have resting on my knee tightly. When did she sit there? I had not even noticed that she was sat next to me. I squeeze her hand back. Not because I am sad that Alex is dead, that I am actually not fussed about. I am glad that he is no longer able to attempt to *move in on my woman*. Why would I be personally fussed about his death when I nearly killed him myself? I would have too if I had not thought he would lead me to his controllers. I squeeze Cindy's hand back because she needs the comfort.

Rosannah and the brothers all sing in harmony. Tears stream down all of their faces apart from Rosannah's.

"Look how brave that woman's being, her voice is incredible," I hear someone say from behind me. It takes a lot to move me, but this song is a pool of emotions. It is being sung with such conviction and I feel a sadness from it. It could be down to the fact that my stunning girlfriend has the most incredible voice.

Cindy sings very off key next to me, pulling me from my thoughts. Vladimir appears to have failed in telling her that now she is a vampire she has the muscle control to be able to sing pitch perfect even if she was tone deaf when human. I make a mental note to tell him when I get the opportunity.

Rosannah and the brothers sing the last line and finish the song. They are greeted with pure silence. I look around the room and see that there is not a dry eye in the place with the exceptions of us vampires. Even the stoic butler is stood by the door with tears running down his cheeks.

A small man in the front row stands up and starts clapping confidently and soon everyone is standing and joining in. Cindy and I stand with our hands still joined. I do not have the heart to yank mine back. I must be going soft. Once the applause has finished we all sit back down and the clergyman begins to end the service. Rosannah comes and sits back down and fortunately Cindy has let go of my hand to wrap her up in a big hug.

"You were *amazing*!" she squeals. Once the service has ended, the small man comes up to Rosannah with a woman who is almost four times his size.

"We're Alex's parents. I just want to thank you on behalf of the family for your beautiful singing, Alex would have loved it," the woman says bursting into tears and grabbing Rosannah in a hug. The small man and Cindy lightly grab her shoulders and leads her away. Rosannah and I watch as Alex's brothers lift Alex's casket and take it outside with their parents and Cindy following. Some of the attendees take the time to tell Rosannah how lovely her singing was. We all follow outside and get into our vehicles.

We let the other cars lead us to our next destination and Rosannah and I travel in silence. After driving for fifteen minutes we pull into a small graveyard and park up near the road. Everyone then makes their way to a freshly dug plot. The clergyman is already here and fortunately holds a very short ceremony but Alex's mother screams in emotional torment as his casket is lowered into the ground. The clergyman leaves and the grave diggers wait to cover the coffin.

"Excuse me everyone," Alex's father says, addressing everyone. "As you can see we're not feeling up for the wake. You're all more than welcome to go to it if you'd like to, or not, but we're now leaving. Thank you as much for coming to give Alex the send-off he deserves," he says and then leads his wife away. A murmur spreads around everyone with half of the attendees heading to the wake and the other half going home.

"What do you want to do?" I ask Rosannah. She turns to me with a worried expression.

"I want to go home," she says. "Cindy," she calls out. Cindy walks over to us.

"Thank you both so much." She smiles at us.

"We're going to head home," Rosannah says with a light smile.

"Oh, no worries Rosannah. You've been so wonderful today. Thank you again," she says and pulls us both into a hug. She lets us go and goes over to Vladimir. They head to their car hand in hand and drive off.

CHAPTER FIFTEEN

Rosannah

The journey back from Alex's burial is a quiet one. Raphael doesn't even play any music in the car. I don't know why he's silent, but I don't have a lot to say after Alex's funeral. Soon we park up outside my building and head up to my apartment. Once inside I sit on the couch with Marmalade and Raphael follows.

"Rosannah, are you okay?" He asks me. "You have been very quiet."

"Today was just emotionally draining and I can't even cry about it," I say with a frown.

"There are things you can no longer do but there is so much more that you are now capable of," he says softly.

"Raphael, why do you speak the way you do? The way you speak sometimes sounds quite old fashioned."

"Ah, I have wondered when you would ask me this question. I was born many years ago and although I have dropped words that have fallen out of the English language I am still in the habit of speaking the way I used to. I am not particularly fond of abbreviations but there are times when they slip in."

"If that's the case then why is it that Lawrence, Nicholas, and Evangeline not speak the same way?" I ask.

"They moved completely with the times. I on the other hand wanted to keep a hold of something from my past. In another three hundred years I hope to still be speaking this way, but I know that some of the way I speak will have been dropped. I cannot stand out too much," he says. A strange feeling settles in my stomach.

"I can't think about being around that long," I admit.

"Well, you certainly will be. You will be around forever."

"Thank goodness I will be with you," I say.

"I would not have it any other way," he says and I can't help but smile brightly. Marmalade meows and jumps off of my lap. She takes a perch on the window sill and curls up into a fluffy ball.

"I don't like the fact that you can't die," I say.

"Excuse me?" Raphael asks with raised eyebrows. Huh? Oh!

"I mean you vampires in general, not you in particular.," I say with a giggle. Raphael doesn't see the funny side and scowls at me.

"You need to stop thinking of us as different, you are vampire too," he says sternly.

"I know that, oh boy do I know it. I have a problem with the fact that there's no getting rid of vampires apart from the space thing. How can nature abandon a species like that?" I say.

"We are a freak of nature, something that slipped through the net so to speak."

"Surely there must be a way?" I ask slightly exasperated, not at Raphael, but at nature.

"If there is anything that can kill us I am yet to come across it."

"That maybe true, but I believe mother nature always finds a way in the end," I say with a sigh.

"Where has this come from?" Raphael asks with a concerned expression.

"The idea of forever doesn't sit right with me. I know that I will exist forever now and there's apparently nothing I can do about it. I've come to terms with it, but I still don't like it," I admit. Raphael gives me a knowing look and takes me into his arms. After a while in silence Raphael pulls back, takes my hands in his and looks at me with a deathly serious expression.

"Rosannah, there is something I would like to ask you," he says nervously. I gasp and I'm slightly weirded out by the fact that my heart doesn't beat speedily. It doesn't beat at all, no matter what I feel. I think it will take a little getting used to. Oh Jeez, I know that vampires get married, but is he actually going to propose? He's not getting down on one knee, not that he has to, but he has taken my hands in his.

"Rosannah, will you move in with me?" He asks looking extremely worried. The relief that flows through me is incredible, but mixed in there is disappointment. Until I met Raphael I'd never really thought about marriage. Why would I? Before him I was never interested in any of the guys I'd met. Thinking about marriage just never occurred to me. I think I probably blanked it out with my mother telling me to marry rich then divorce to get money. It's just so disgusting and maybe I knew deep down that if I ever married for love, my mother would do nothing but bitch about it. 'Oh Rosannah, how are you and *the man* doing?' There's no way she would acknowledge any husband I had out of love. Raphael rubs the backs of my hands to get my attention. Oh right, I'm meant to give him an answer. I can't think of any reasons apart from two that would be a problem.

"What about Marmalade?" I ask.

"She can come too," he replies encouragingly.

"What about my mother? She's going to be a nightmare."

"I will sort her out, do not worry about that at all." Well, that's the problems sorted out. There's only one thing left to do.

"Yes! I will move in with you," I say and go to jump up. Raphael pulls me back down gently.

"There is just one more thing I should tell you," he says with worry etched into in his face.

"Rosannah, I did not just want a valuation done when you first came to my home. In fact, I did not want an evaluation done at all. It was simply a rouse to get you to my home. I had spotted you one day and I was attracted to you. Maybe I misinterpreted my attraction, but I had originally wanted to do bad things to you. I brainwashed Marie and set everything in motion. Harry turned up and got some things moving much quicker than I had planned," he admits.

"Raphael, I must say that I am shocked that you went to such lengths to get me to your home, but I am certainly not shocked that you wanted to do bad things to me." I laugh. Raphael looks dumbfounded.

"You are not angry with me?"

"Why would I be?" I ask incredulously.

"Because of what I intended to do," he says clearly confused.

"You were quite wicked to me at times. I spent the first part of my time in your house thinking you were completely insane. Then I found out what you were, which explained a lot when taking into account your history, but over time I saw that there was good in you. I accepted you for who you actually were and fell in love with you already knowing your flaws. I know why you were the way you were, jaded from years of existence and being forced to face the prospect of forever. It's how you came to terms with it. You didn't have anything to make you feel anything other than what you felt." I say.

"Oh," he says.

"I best phone my mother," I say and go to the phone. I pick it up but it's dead. I look down and see it's not plugged in. Plugging it in I look sheepishly at Raphael. He gives me a knowing look. Strange. I speed dial my mum but it rings and rings. It never rings more than once. Something's up. After seven rings she answers.

"Rosannah, I don't know why you even bother ringing me. You just can't be bothered with me at all," she says dramatically down the line.

"Mum, I've been busy and before you say it, no I'm not a drug dealer or a lesbian." I hear Raphael laugh and fight back one myself. "I wanted to tell you that I'm moving."

"Why on Earth would you be moving? Ah, you're moving in with your girlfriend!" Oh God, she is beyond ridiculous.

"No mum, I've already told you. I'm not a lesbian, I have a boyfriend and I'm moving in with him. I want to let my flat out," I say.

"Stop lying to me Rosannah!" she hollers down the phone at me.

"I just knew you would understand mother. You can meet him soon. Bye" I say and hang up. The phone starts ringing and I pull the plug out again. "That went well," I say sarcastically turning to Raphael. He's in front of me instantly.

"Let us focus on moving you and deal with your mother later. When would you like to move?" he asks me.

"Now?"

"Wait here, let me get some boxes and muscle power," he says and dashes off. Ten minutes later he returns with Lawrence, Nicholas, Evangeline and a ton of boxes. They all look to me for instructions.

"Erm, okay, Evangeline you can do the bathroom, Nicholas you do the kitchen, Lawrence and Raphael you do the front room and hallways and I'll do my bedroom. Pile the boxes up in the middle of the floor in your designated rooms and please watch out for Marmalade."

We all dash around at speed and have the whole place wrapped up in five minutes flat.

"Now to get this all moved over to mine. Nicholas, you can take your boxes to my kitchen, Evangeline, to my en-suite bathroom. Rosannah to my bedroom and Lawrence and I will take our boxes to my TV room," he instructs. We all dash over to Raphael's and place our boxes. Lawrence, Nicholas and Evangeline head home and Raphael and I head back to my flat. I've left my furniture and appliances because I won't need them and I want to rent the flat out furnished. I think I may offer it to Paul, unless

Nicholas and Brianna want to move and live above her mum. I pick up Marmalade, put her in her travel box and hand her to Raphael so I can lock up my flat. We head down to Raphael's car and once we're in and Marmalade is secured Raphael pulls away pitting his foot down. Marmalade meows in protest.

"Raphael, you'll have to drive a little slower for Marmalade," I warn.

"Ah yes, sorry Marmalade," he apologises.

Once at Raphael's I let out Marmalade and she has a little sniff around. We follow her into the TV room and she hops up onto a chair that is obviously used more than the others. Digging her claws in she settles down and falls asleep.

"That is typical. She has picked my favourite chair," Raphael says with a smile.

After Raphael and I have sorted through my belongings and put things away, we come back to the TV room. Marmalade is still in the same place fast asleep.

"Well, she's definitely settled in," I smile. "Have you spoken to Marie yet?"

"I have not. Are you planning on returning to work?" Raphael asks and puts his arms around me.

"I'd like to," I say.

"I will do it now and tell them that you are on holiday until next week. I will brainwash them to accept your new appearance. Then I will go and to talk to Mathias again. I hope that this time I can get him to see sense." He gives me a quick kiss on the lips and runs off.

CHAPTER SIXTEEN

Raphael

After leaving Rosannah at our home, I arrive at her work. It takes me minutes to brainwash the relevant people with a made up story. I then head to Mathias's. The door opens as I approach it and I dash into his living room.

"Are you alone?" I ask, referring to his wife.

"Yes. Now what do I owe to the pleasure of your company?" Asks Mathias.

"I do not think I need to explain why I am here but I can if it is necessary," I reply.

"Oh not this again! I would prefer it if you didn't bring your spits with Reggie here." Mathias sighs.

"Mathias, I will only try this one last time. Rosannah was taken with the intention of being killed. She was turned into a vampire against her will and the one responsible for all of this is Reggie." I say as calmly as I can.

"I still cannot believe Reggie would do such a thing." An uncontrollable roar breaks out of me and Mathias backs away.

"Do you not trust me?" I ask as I stalk forward.

"Yes I do but ..."

"Have I not been loyal enough?"

"You have but ..."

"I know your biggest secret! How can you not trust my word when I have kept the fact that you can be killed a secret for years!" I yell. I see the defeat in Mathias's face.

"You are right Raph." Mathias says with a sigh. Suddenly the front door bursts open and Reggie appears in the front room door way.

"What an interesting discovery I have just made. Well you two kept quite the secret to yourselves. How selfish of you to not share such information, Raphael. Well, I'm certainly glad you have now." Reggie says with a laugh. His face turns serious and he glares at Mathias. "For what it's worth, Raphael was telling you the truth about me changing Rosannah and there's nothing you can do about it. I had come here to tell you a load of lies, but it looks like I don't need to now because you'll be dead! Your time will be up soon old man," he says to Mathias who looks petrified. "Speaking of dead, how is Rosannah doing?" he asks me with a sneer. I go to go after him but Mathias stops me. Again, I have to push dealing with Reggie aside.

"You are now no longer safe. You have to come with me," I say to Mathias and pull my phone out before he can argue with me. Pressing speed dial I call Lawrence.

"What's up bro?" He answers.

"I need you to get Nicholas and head to mine. Do not involve Evangeline." I instruct.

"Is everything okay?" he asks.

"No, it is not, but I will explain everything when I see you," I say and hang up. "Let us get going." I tell Mathias.

"Wait, I must call my wife," Mathias says. He pulls out a phone and calls her. "Darling, I will be staying away for a while, lads break. There's also been an accident. Could you arrange to get the front door replaced?"

"We just replaced it after the last time Reggie came over!" I hear her whinge down the phone.

"I know; this should be the last time." Mathias tries to reason.

"Why do I not believe that! I'll get it sorted!" she says. The line goes dead and Mathias looks sheepishly at me.

"Come on." I say and dash off.

CHAPTER SEVENTEEN

Rosannah

Lawrence and Nicholas come in the front door looking concerned.

"You two look worried, is everything okay?" I ask them.

"Something has happened, but all we know is that we need to wait here for Raphael and Mathias," says Lawrence. What could have happened? I don't have to wait long. Soon an angry Raphael and a terrified Mathias arrive. Without a word we all head into the TV room. Everyone ends up staring at Marmalade who is still curled up asleep on Raphael's chair.

"So your own brother isn't allowed in your precious chair but the cat is?" Asks Lawrence.

"I like the cat more than I like you," he says.

"Raphael!" I chastise him.

"What? It is true," he says.

"Can you at least tell us what's going on?" I ask.

"Something very bad has happened, but first I need to explain something to you," Raphael says addressing the twins. "May I?" He asks Mathias. He nods his consent. "Mathias is the only vampire that can be killed." The twins laugh for some time but soon realise that Raphael is serious. "Oh," I say, pretending to be shocked. I wasn't meant to know about this so I play ignorant.

"No way Raph!" says Lawrence.

"How is that even possible?" Asks Nicholas.

"It is a long story, but essentially Mathias became the first vampire nearly seven thousand years ago. He is destructible but went on to create the indestructible vampire. I was the only other to know this apart from Mathias himself but now Reggie knows thanks to me yelling it and Reggie being within the area."

"Raph, you idiot." Lawrence laughs.

"Seven thousand years?" Asks a bewildered Nicholas.

"Yes, Nicholas. Lawrence I did not know Reggie was there, but that is not the point. The point now is that Mathias is in danger. Reggie has vowed to kill Mathias at some point," Raphael says regretfully.

"Is there nothing that vampire won't do?" Asks an angry Lawrence.

"I would prefer that the rest of The Synod or anyone else doesn't know," says Mathias, ignoring what Lawrence just said.

"We definitely have to keep this from Evangeline then," says Nicholas.

"Rosannah, I owe you a huge apology. I am sorry that I did not believe you. I thought I knew Reggie; he was like a son to me. Could you find it in your heart to forgive me?" Mathias asks.

"Of course." I reply. Raphael growls and I glare at him.

"Now you all know that we have to keep Mathias safe. He has told his wife that he is staying away for a while. He is going to stay here while we figure out how to sort out Reggie once and for all and to keep him safe," Raphael says.

"How can we sort Reggie out if we can't tell The Synod?" asks Nicholas.

"Leave that to me, all you need to do is stay here for the time being," says Raphael. What could he possibly have planned?

CHAPTER EIGHTEEN

Raphael

I've shown Mathias to a spare room and now I am resting on my bed. I plan to attempt to change Mathias into an indestructible vampire. I have tried to convince Mathias to let me try from when he first revealed his secret to me. He has been dead set against it, but I am hoping Regius' death threat will be enough this time. If not, Mathias will stay here until he agrees. He cannot go anywhere without bodyguards now.

"Raph!" Lawrence yells from the TV room.

"What is it?" I yell from my bedroom.

"I think you want to get down here!" He yells. With a light growl I head to where the twins are standing with Mathias and Rosannah. We look out of the TV room window across my front lawn to see Harry walking towards us.

"Now isn't the time for him to visit, surely?" asks Nicholas.

"Nicholas..." I start to say when Harry rushes at my front door and smashes through it. "No one smashes my front door but me!" I shout as we all rush out into the hall.

"I see you're looking better than the last time I saw you," Harry says to Rosannah.

"When the hell did he become a vampire?" asks a confused Lawrence.

"A little while ago now, but it's irrelevant. I'm here for the old man. It's time to die," Harry says.

"What on Earth will Reggie get from Mathias's death?" I ask.

"Well, I shouldn't tell you anything, but I suppose it won't hurt. Reggie wants to dissolve The Synod. With Mathias gone, The Synod will collapse. I'm guessing you don't know that if the current leader doesn't assign someone to take over when they are no longer able to be in charge then The Synod is no more. You wouldn't because the only circumstance that would have ensured an indestructible vampire could no longer be the leader of The Synod would be if they committed a crime punishable by space ejection. Mathias counted on the fact that his little secret would be safe and was stupid enough not to select a second in command."

"He can pick someone now!" Says Lawrence.

"Stupid, stupid Lawrence. The rest of The Synod has to be involved," he says with a big smile.

"What if this situation ever happened? How could The Synod carry on?" asks Nicholas.

"It won't continue. That's the point. It's a stupid way of doing things and it's all Mathias's fault," says Harry.

"Why would you do this to The Synod, to us, to Rosannah? After all The Synod has done for you, this is how you repay us?" asks Mathias. Harry aggressively moves forward and we all push Mathias backto keep him from Harry's reach.

"All you have done for me? You must be joking right? I was everyone's bitch. I did what I could to ensure some of you did your jobs properly. Everyone I raised an issue with dismissed me like a piece of shit. If I wasn't dismissed, I was brainwashed. You had no right to treat me in such a way!" Harry yells.

"You were the only human to be a part of The Synod. The plan was to one day have you become a vampire. I saw great potential in you," admits Mathias.

"Are you serious Mathias? Did you lose your mind along with your body parts?" I turn and ask him.

"What is wrong with me being a vampire?" asks Harry.

"Everything!" I yell, turning back.

"I think what Raphael is trying to say is that we needed to make sure you could be trusted. We don't just change people," Mathias says.

"I had been a part of The Synod for twenty-seven years. That's long enough!" Harry yells.

"Yes, I quite agree. Twenty-seven years is twenty-seven years too long," I growl.

"This isn't getting us anywhere. All I want to know is why you double crossed us?" Asks Mathias.

"I would have thought it was obvious, but I'll explain it again before I kill you. The Synod treated me like shit and Reggie came along and promised me what I had wanted for a long time. I was rewarded with eternal life in exchange for helping him carry out his plans. I got changed sooner than planned because Alex couldn't bring Rosannah to us, so once I was a vampire I was able to get Rosannah," he says.

"You traded my life so that you could become a vampire?" Asks Rosannah as she slowly walks towards Harry. Her voice is small but clipped. Rosannah is beyond angry. Harry smiles a cocky smile at her and she launches herself at him. He is waiting for her and grabs her by the shoulders as she reaches him. Ignoring his grip, she grabs him by the throat. What happens next has the rest of us shocked.

CHAPTER NINETEEN

Rosannah

As I reach Harry he grabs me by my shoulders. I fling his arms off of me and grab him by the throat. I growl at him as I squeeze with all of my might. It's some time before I feel a hand on my right shoulder. I whip my head around and see it's Raphael. His eyes are wide and he looks shocked to the core. Is it not a good thing for a female vampire to attack another? Have I embarrassed myself? Embarrassed him? Is he disgusted with me? Raphael swallows hard.

"You can let go of Harry now," he says, almost whispering. I look at Harry and realise that he doesn't look right. His eyes are wide with fear and are staring off in the distance behind me. Finally, my brain tells my hand to let go of him. As I let go Harry's head drops like a heavy stone and rolls off stopping at Lawrence's feet, who coils away from it. I look down and see Harry's body in a crumpled heap on the floor. I have no idea what has happened and I look at the twins and Mathias who are gobsmacked. I turn to Raphael.

"What the ...?" I ask.

"I do not know how, but you grabbed him by the throat so hard that you detached his head from his body," he says. I stare at him for a while but then the strangest thing happens. I have the biggest urge to laugh. Slowly it bubbles up. It starts as a tiny giggle but soon morphs into an enormous cackle.

"I detached his head?" I laugh. "I actually killed an indestructible vampire?" I cackle. "That is hilarious, you can get up now Harry, play time is over," I say in between laughs. I prod his body with my right foot and my laughs die out. "Come on, stop playing games, Harry! Get up!" I yell. "HARRY!" I scream.

"Rosannah, he is not getting back up" he says gently. Now it is my turn to be gobsmacked. Slowly I start to cry dry tears. Raphael gingerly reaches out to me but I dash off to my old room. I stop by the window. Soon sobs wrack through my body. It's not long before all the others join me.

"Rosannah, are you okay?" Asks Raphael. I turn to him and he looks petrified.

"Do I look okay?" I ask stalking towards him. "I never meant to kill him!"

"We all know that," Raphael says backing up from me a little.

"I just killed an indestructible vampire and I can't even cry about it!" I yell.

"We are just as shocked as you are."

"But now you're all going to be scared of me," I say.

"Well, that may be true, but I have to admit that I do find the super vampire thing quite attractive," Raphael whispers as he edges closer to me. I glare at him.

"Seriously Raph. You are aware that she is fully capable of ripping your dick off right?" asks Lawrence. I look down at Raphael's crotch with feigned determination and he covers himself up with his hands and makes an uncharacteristic high pitched sound.

"That is not the issue at hand. We have Regius hell bent on killing Mathias," says Raphael.

"I say we let killer here at him," says Nicholas. Raphael winces at his words as he drops his hands.

"If that isn't tact then I don't know what is," says Lawrence.

"I second Nicholas," I say, ignoring Lawrence and much to Raphael's surprise.

"It is just as easy to eject him into space," Raphael says.

"No it's not. It's a bitch to get any vampire..." Raphael clamps a hand over Nicholas's mouth to shut him up.

"We will discuss this later. Right now let us give Rosannah some time to process everything," says Raphael. Mathias goes to complain but Raphael glares at him then smiles at me. Giving me a quick kiss on the lips he is gone followed by the others. I hear footsteps as they dash across the front lawn. I head over to Raphael room and flop down onto the bed. Rolling onto my back I stare at the ceiling and let everything that just happened sink in.

CHAPTER TWENTY
Raphael

Everyone follows me to Lawrence's house. Once there he lets us all in.

"We did just see Rosannah kill a vampire right?" he asks.

"Yes. We saw her use her brute strength to crush Harry's neck so much that his head came off," I reply.

"How is that even possible?" Asks Mathias.

"I have no idea, but this changes everything. It changes our history, our beliefs and our very existence," I reply.

"Well I don't think any of us should piss her off, like ever" says Nicholas.

"I second that," says Lawrence.

"I am not sure what to do about Regius at this moment in time, but I think it is time to see if I can turn you into one of us," I tell Mathias. He pulls a face and I know it has not settled very well with him.

"I don't see why Rosannah can't protect me," he says.

"Let me get this straight, rather than see if you can become indestructible you want Rosannah to essentially protect you for eternity?" I ask.

"She has proven that she is certainly more than capable," he responds.

"She does not exist to be your babysitter!" I yell.

"So what Raphael is trying to say is that Rosannah will not be looking after you," says Lawrence.

"What I am saying is that it is time that Mathias became the guinea pig." Mathias thinks about it for a while. "This is ridiculous. Either you try to become one of us or choose death by the hands of Regius. Those are the only options you have. Even if we eject him into space we will have no idea who and how many he may have told about your ability to be killed. No one will be able to guarantee your safety and there is no way Rosannah will be your protector," I warn him.

"Okay," Mathias says in defeat. "You can try to change me. No offence Lawrence and Nicholas but I'd rather it was Raph."

"None taken," They say in unison.

"Do we need to do anything that involves the rest of The Synod?" I ask Mathias.

"No, you have my word that this will be okay," he says. Before he can change his mind I bite my wrist and his neck. Putting my wound to his, the blood mingles and the damage is healed within split seconds.

"It is done," I say. After a few minutes Mathias doubles over and screams in pain. It is not long before Mathias crumples to his knees, but he continues to scream in agony. This lasts for about ten minutes as we all watch. It may sound cruel, but there really is nothing that we can possibly do for him. Even though he is already a vampire and his body does not need to go through as much change as a human, it appears that he has not been paralysed during the change nor has he lost consciousness. Finally, the screaming stops and eventually he manages to stand up with help from Lawrence and Nicholas. We patently wait as it takes a while for him to speak.

"That was the most painful experience I have ever had in my seven thousand years. I pray that it worked," he says.

"Well, there's only way to find out," says Lawrence.

"I never thought I'd ever say this but Raphael, would you pull my arm off please? If this has worked you won't be able to, but if it hasn't, I should be able to reattach it."I grab his hand but Lawrence stops me.

"Can we do this outside please? If this has worked then when you do pull him he will go flying, and although I'm all up for seeing if this has been successful, I don't want my house smashed up," Lawrence says.

"Excellent point," I say and we all head outside. Nicholas and Lawrence check our surroundings and once they give the all clear I take Mathias's hand again. "Brace yourself," I warn him, and once I can see he is ready I pull as hard as I can on his arm. Mathias ends up being flung thirty foot but manages to land and steady himself like a cat. I look at my hand and I am relieved to see that it is empty. Mathias stands and turns to me with his eyes closed.

"Did it work?" He asks.

"Open your eyes," I tell him. Slowly he opens them and looks down at his hands. "It worked!" He yells.

"You truly are one of us." I smile. "Now you are safe."

"Unless you piss Rosannah off." Lawrence laughs. I glare at him but Nicholas steps forward.

"That's all well and good, but we have Regius to sort out. I still say we let Rosannah at him, take her right to his door step."

"May I make a suggestion?" asks Mathias.

"You may," I tell him.

"Reggie has no idea what's happened to Harry. At some point he's going to assume that he's done a runner so it will only be a matter of time before he turns up to *finish* me off himself. If he attacks me and he is killed by Rosannah we won't need to involve The Synod beforehand. No rules would have been broken. In all honesty, I don't know if the rest of The Synod can be fully trusted, so I would prefer it if they didn't know about any of this yet," he admits.

"I agree. We keep this between us and wait for Regius to strike. It will be down as self-defence and we can all act as if Regius's death is a shock to all of us if it is ever questioned," I say.

"Although there are some who will query Regius' whereabouts, no one will ever suspect that he was killed unless we start to tell and show people so I doubt we will ever have to tell the rest of The Synod," says Lawrence.

"Good point. Are we all agreed?" I ask.

"Yes," they all reply.

"Let us get back to Rosannah and see if she is happy with our plan," I say and we all dash back to my home. I head upstairs and find Rosannah on our bed staring at the ceiling.

"Did you manage to sort anything out?" She asks as she gets up.

"Mathias is now indestructible," I say.

"That's great news," Rosannah smiles but soon it turns into a frown.

"What about Reggie?" she asks.

"We have a plan but it relies on you. If you do not want any part of it we will understand," I say gently.

"What's this plan?" She asks.

"We want let Regius come to us and let him attack. He will come here eventually thinking Harry has deserted him. It is then that you can kill him. No one else will need to know and neither will anyone be suspicious," I say.

"Your plan sounds like a great one." She smiles.

"It is Mathias's plan," I say.

"What about The Synod? Surely they should be informed at some point," she says.

"They are currently being kept in the dark over this. Mathias is unsure of who he can trust out of them after Regius' betrayal," I say.

"I understand." She smiles. I take her by the hand and we head downstairs to meet the others. We gather around Harry's body.

"What are we going to do about this?" asks Lawrence.

"I suggest we hide it. We do not want anyone other than us knowing that Harry is dead. Agreed?" I ask.

"Agreed," everyone replies.

"I'm going to head home now," says Mathias.

"I do not think that is a good idea. Regius will expect you to be in our care. If we did this at your home your wife could then possibly be a witness," I say.

"You are right Raphael. I didn't think about that at all," he says.

"You can stay with me," says Lawrence. "I will call everyone as soon as anything happens."

"I'll stay with you too," Nicholas adds.

"Okay, that is fine with me," I say.

"What about Brianna?" Asks Rosannah.

"She will be fine." He smiles at me.

"If we're all decided then we better head off," says Lawrence and he dashes off with Mathias and Nicholas. Rosannah looks down at Harry's body with disgust.

"I will deal with this," I say as I gather him up. I head outside and down into the crypt.

"Sorry Uncle Frederic," I say as I open his coffin. A skeleton in rags greets me as I dump Harry in with it. I seal the coffin and head back up to Rosannah.

CHAPTER TWENTY-ONE

Rosannah

Raphael soon appears.

"Should I even ask what you did with him?" I ask.

"He is in a coffin, sharing with my uncle," he says with a grim smile.

"Eww," I say pulling a face. Raphael laughs.

"What?" I ask.

"It is you," he says as he takes me in his arms.

"Me? What about me?" I ask, suddenly feeling self-conscious.

"You truly are amazing. How you have handled everything. You have handled becoming a vampire better than any vampire I have ever known by far and now you are able to kill me in more ways than one. Who would have thought that you would be the one who could end our existence? I am completely in awe of you," he whispers.

"This isn't right," I say.

"What do you mean?" He asks, perplexed.

"I shouldn't be the one who can kill vampires. If anyone should be able to it should be you!" I say. Raphael is so much more deserving of this ability than I am. It is then an idea enters my head.

"Nature chose you," he says with his eyebrows furrowing.

"What if we can get mother nature to spread the love?" I ask.

"Spread the love?" He asks confused.

"Yes, what if I try to change you?" I ask. Raphael's eyes go wide.

"You want to try and change me?" He asks slightly worried.

"Yes, who else is better than you?" I say.

"But this is your gift, it is not mine," he says.

"Why shouldn't it be yours too? Why can't we be equal in every way?" I ask.

"I do not know about this Rosannah."

"Think about it. You could actually deal out death to vampires as a proper punishment too," I say.

"Space is a proper punishment," he says.

"That may be true, but death would be quicker and more efficient. It would send waves of fear through the vampire world."

"We do not even know if this would work," Raphael says with worry. He really is trying to talk me out of this, but I am certain this is the way forward. Raphael doesn't know his potential.

"Are you frightened?" I ask.

"My main reason for refusing is because this is your special ability, but I must admit that I am a little bit scared. A wrong move on your part could kill me," he says. I realise that he is correct. I certainly don't want to hurt or kill him.

"You'll have to show me how it's done."

"Okay," he says in resign. "I will let you try. It has to be done very fast because of the rate we heal at. You need to bite your wrist and then bite me and place the wounds together so that your blood can enter my body. It is a preference to bite the neck but you may choose my wrist instead if you would like, but try biting your wrist first and see how that goes."

"Will this hurt?" I ask holding my wrist up.

"No, you will feel something pierce your skin but it will not hurt at all."

"How do I even get my teeth to come down?" I ask.

"Just think about it, like changing your eye colour."

I do as he suggests and concentrate on my teeth. I feel them descend. It feels quite alien to me, it's something I'll just have to get used to. Steadying myself I sink my teeth into my wrist. Raphael is right, it doesn't hurt at all. I pull my wrist away and watch it heal almost instantly. I repeat this several times and get the knack of biting through vampire skin.

"Right, are you ready?" I ask Raphael and step towards him. He holds his hands up and backs away slightly.

"Look, you must be sure not to bite too deeply and to open your jaw back up when you pull away from me," he says.

"Duly noted, now come here so I can bite you," I say. He sheepishly walks to me. "Head to side," I instruct.

"Which side would you prefer?" he asks.

"Hmmm, your left side I think." I reply with a grin. Raphael tilts his head to his right and I steady myself. *1...2...3...* With that, I bite my wrist, bite Raphael's neck, and put the two wounds together.

"Did it work?" I ask, hopeful.

"I am afraid that definitely will not work. Your wrist was healed before it reached my neck," he says.

"How can you be sure?" I ask, my bubble popped.

"I watched it heal, you must do it faster," he smiles sympathetically. I then proceed to try once more and fail again.

"Why isn't this working?" I yell in frustration.

"Try it as fast as you can," Raphael suggests. Taking his advice, that is exactly what I do.

"Did it work this time?" I ask but Raphael holds up a finger to me to ask for a minute and then doubles over.

"Oh my God, are you alright?" I ask.

"I am okay, but damn this is painful!" he says through gritted teeth. He lowers himself to the ground and lies down on the floor. "Is there anything I can do?" I ask. It's a stupid question, but I have to offer him help.

"Hold my hand," he says as he starts to growl in pain. I stay there with him, holding his hand while he yells out in pain for some time. I don't know how long it takes, but night time falls before he stops crying out in pain.

"Can you get up?" I ask him gently. In an instant he's up, pulling me up with him and takes me in his arms.

"Thank you," he whispers in my ear.

"We don't know if it's worked yet," I say.

"No, not for that. For being here with me while I went through that agony. It reminded me of when I became a vampire. I had you with me this time, thank you!" he says. *Now I understand.* We hold each other until Raphael pulls away from me.

"I would love to just stay here and hold you, but I think we should check if this has worked," he says. Nodding in agreement I take his hand in mine.

"Let me know if it starts to hurt at all," I say. When Raphael nods I slowly start to squeeze. I continue to squeeze and get no reaction so I keep going until I am using my full strength. In a flood of relief, I let him go and give him a huge hug. "It worked!" I yell.

"I need to actually try my strength out," he says.

"You will be able to try it on Regius," I say.

"As much as I would like to, I do not think I am ready to tell the others just yet. There have been so many revelations and deceit recently that I would prefer to wait."

"I understand," I say with a smile.

CHAPTER TWENTY-TWO

Raphael

Last night was certainly an emotional one for me. I am now a vampire that is capable of killing another. I lay in bed with Rosannah laid across my chest, lightly stroking her hair while I ponder this. My phone beeps, grabbing my attention. Within seconds I am out of bed and I have read the message.

"Rosannah, we must head to Lawrence's. Reggie has turned up," I say. In no time we are dressed and dash over to Lawrence's. We arrive at his house to find the front door open and everyone in the living room.

"Ah, I knew you wouldn't be too far. Do you know just how brown your nose is? I bet if I looked at that old fool's ass hole it would be shaped just like your beak!" Regius spits at me. Rage flows through me, but I know I must keep my anger under control.

"Seriously, can we leave Mathias's ass hole out of this please? It's pretty gross," complains Lawrence.

"Yes, the ever faithful whining idiot. Well at least you're reliable, I suppose. Can you believe that Harry has done a runner on me? I gave him the gift of immortality and he repays me by going AWOL."

"Oh how inconvenient for you," says Nicholas sarcastically.

"At least you understand, albeit in that demented mind of yours. Alex was a failure; Harry was a failure. Rather than waste time I should have just done everything myself," Regius says.

"If you think you are going to kill Mathias then it is you who is demented!" I yell.

"Dear Raphael. You think that you are the big almighty. I get that you want to be top dog, but Mathias is never going to step aside for you to take over and once he's gone there will be no more Synod. You won't even be able to punish me because The Synod will have dissolved."

"Do you really think that the other members will allow you to get away with everything you have done? Synod or not, they have morals!" I yell.

"Morals? Good God Raphael, you are so dense! It will be of no surprise to you that I was one of the vampires who attacked your family, but what if I was to tell you another Synod member was right there too. That leaves two, do you really think they would have the ability help you?" He asks.

"You lie!" I yell.

"And what is it I'd gain from lying? I'm sure if you confronted them they'd admit it! They have no reason to fear you, especially if The Synod has crumbled! They will receive no punishment."

"Why are you telling me this?" I ask.

"I couldn't before because I couldn't get The Synod dissolved. Even if I had managed to get Mathias done for some heinous crime that would have seen him ejected into space, a successor would have been picked, but now that Mathias can be killed I can. I know Mathias won't want the others knowing about his indiscretion so he won't be picking a successor. Like I said, there's nothing you can actually do now.

You have been hunting down the one who changed you all this time. I am the one who changed you. The other name you are looking for in reference to your family being killed and changed is Bernadette." Shock flows around the room.

"You can ask her about her involvement later, but for now I have a death sentence to deliver first," Regius says as he steps forward.

"Do you really think you have gotten away with everything you've done?" asks Rosannah who steps in front of Regius. Lawrence and Nicholas take a notable step backwards.

"What are you talking about? I already have you imbecile!" he says. I wince at his words because I know what Rosannah is capable of and they would not have gone down well with her.

"No you haven't!" She yells.

"What the hell can you do? Nothing! There's nothing anyone can do! I have done what I wanted and have gotten away with it and I shall continue to do so. How dare you disrespect me in such a way! You should be thanking me, I made you, and your stupid boyfriend! I gave you forever with your lover boy over there, although I'd seriously question his relations with a certain old cretin!" I cringe at his words because I know Rosannah must be seething. She reaches out and grabs his arm and Nicholas and Lawrence move back even further.

"What is this? Do you really want to fight me? You cannot hurt me!" Regius laughs. He tries to pull his arm back but he cannot get it to budge. The smile soon turns into frustration. Mathias races off and leaves. I assume he does not want to watch Regius die.

"Let go of me you filthy piece of trash!" Regius yells at Rosannah. With a deep growl Rosannah pulls on Regius arm with a sharp tug. His arm comes clean off and a look of utter terror creases his features. Rosannah drops the limb and Regius dashes off grabbing it in the process.

"There is no way on this Earth you are getting away!" Rosannah screams and she gives chase. All of us follow, but Rosannah is too fast.

Regius frantically runs not knowing where he is going. Erratically, he runs through crowds of people, trees, and buildings. While Regius narrowly misses them, Rosannah gives them a wider berth.

"Rosannah!" I yell after her, worried about what people may see if she catches him within sight of them, but she presses on. Soon we enter a deep forest, much to my relief. Whizzing in and out of trees Regius's panic grows, but something strange happens. Regius slows down and stops. It is as if he giving up. He turns to face Rosannah and lets out an ear piercing scream as she catches up with him. A large amount of birds flees the tree tops. Rosannah slows down, but still moves towards Regius. We all stop chasing but watch from a distance, not knowing what we will see.

When Rosannah reaches Regius a few things happen at once: Rosannah lets out a war cry and skids to a holt as she buries her hands into Regius's chest. He looks at her with shock, his mouth wide-open and in one fail swoop she twists her hands outwards and rips him clean apart. Skin and sinew tears, bones obliterate and body parts fly everywhere. As a result,

Rosannah is covered in blood, shards of bone, and flesh; Regius' mangled remains flop to the floor. Flinging her wrists at the pile of remains in front of her, Rosannah flicks what she can off of her hands and forearms.

"Not so cocky now are you?" she says to the pile of mush. After some time, her shoulders sag and she turns to face us. "I'm not so sure I should have done it like that."

"The world is better off without him trust me," says Nicholas.

"If that's true, then why do I feel guilty?" She asks.

"It's your human nature. Give it a few years and killing won't be a bother to you at all," he says.

"I don't think I could get used to that," she admits as I go and put my arms around her. She places her head against my shoulder, but does not put her arms around me to which I am grateful for.

"Give it time. You do not have to kill anyone but, if you do they would be criminals. Even when we kill we only kill criminals, even though they are human criminals," I tell her.

"Let's get this mess cleaned up. We can't leave him here; the authorities would have a field day if they found the remains of a vampire," says Lawrence.

"What should we do with him?" Asks Nicholas.

"If you can bag him up, I can put him with Harry," I say. Within minutes the twins have raced off, and returned with bags. Looking grimly at what is left of Regius, they fill the bags.

"We'll drop these off at yours," says Nicholas and they are gone.

"I think we should head back home so I can get cleaned up. I don't want *him* on me any longer," Rosannah says and we too race home.

Once home Rosannah goes for her shower and I put the bags containing what is left of Regius, which the twins left in my entryway, in the coffin of my great uncle Julian in the crypt, I head back in to the house and text Mathias to come over. I know why he fled, but he must be told about Regius's death. He is here within minutes. I let him in and lead him to the dining room.

"I am so sorry Raphael," he says.

"It is okay Mathias; I understand why you left." I say.

"Is he...?" He starts.

"Regius is dead," I tell him. A look of sadness shows in his eyes, but it disappears almost instantly.

"Well, at least it is done now," he says. "I know this may sound a bit strange, but is it possible to see him? Say some sort of goodbye?"

"I would not advise it. He is in pieces, literally, but you are welcome to say goodbye if you truly wish."

"Please," he says.

"Follow me," I say and lead him out and down to the crypt. I open up the coffin and Mathias gasps but quickly gathers himself.

"It is a shame you had to take the path you did my dear boy. You have done some truly questionable things, but I will indeed miss you. Goodbye," he says and closes Regius's eyes. I close everything back up and we head back up into the house in silence.

"That must have taken some serious strength for Rosannah to do that amount of damage," Mathias says with a grim expression.

"Do you really want to talk about it?" I ask him. He nods. "Rosannah's hands sliced into his chest like a hot knife through butter."

"How is it even possible for her to be able to do that?" He asks with raised eyebrows.

"I really have no idea. Perhaps one day we will find out. Maybe we will not at all. All I know is that Mother Nature has found a way to rid the world of us," I say thoughtfully.

"We now have a proper way to deal with criminal vampires," says Mathias.

"You would suggest to using Rosannah's ability for the benefit of The Synod? A group of vampires that have so far bore two traitors? I do not think we should use Rosannah in such a way."

"I disagree with you Raphael," says Rosannah who walks into the room. "The Synod may be broken at the moment, but there's no reason why in the future, when everything is sorted, that I can't enforce death sentences."

"I know you are not too happy with killing." I say, giving her a knowing look. I am putting a front up for Mathias's sake.

"If I'm thereto issue serious punishment, then that's what I must do," she says giving me a meaningful look. We need to keep my new transition attempt under wraps. We have no idea if I have the ability to kill other vampires, so it is best we keep this to ourselves until we know for sure.

"So *you're*okay with this?" Mathias asks Rosannah.

"Yes, ultimately," she replies.

"I think we should deal with Bernadette first before we do anything else," I say.

"I am in agreement with you. Sort out Bernadette, you have my full permission to execute her, then we will gather the last members and explain what has been going on. I am highly doubtful that Porticus or Vladimir would have anything to do with this. If they have then they too will be executed," Mathias says. After a nod from me, Mathias races off.

"To Bernadette's," I say.

CHAPTER TWENTY-THREE

Raphael

We arrive at Bernadette's house and she opens the door to us.

"To what do I owe the pleasure?" She asks. "Wait a minute, shouldn't you have a heartbeat?" She asks Rosannah.

"Do not play dumb with us. You know full well that Rosannah has not had a heartbeat for a while," I say.

"What are you talking about?" She asks.

"Your partner in crime, Regius, changed her," I say. Bernadette looks completely confused. It appears to be a genuine reaction.

"You're wrong. There's no way Reggie would have changed her! It must have been you," she says, pointing a finger at me.

"I can assure you that I was not the one who changed her. I knew Rosannah's stance on becoming one of us. If I had changed her it would have been against her will and I would not do that to her."

"When you put it like that I suppose it makes sense, but I don't understand why Reggie would change her," she says with a frown.

"Because it was your understanding that he would kill her," I say through gritted teeth.

"Raphael, I really have no idea what you're talking about," she says but Rosannah growls and steps forward. I hold her back with an arm. "You're kidding me! You seriously think you can hurt me?" Bernadette laughs. I have to increase my strength to keep Rosannah back and eventually she pulls back.

"You, Rosannah and I all know that you were working with Regius," I accuse.

"Alright, I admit it. There really isn't a lot you can do about it. The rest of The Synod won't believe you anyway," she says with a shrug of her shoulders.

"Mathias knows everything," I say as calmly as I can.

"He knows nothing!" she yells.

"He knows you used Alex to try and get Rosannah and when that failed you both resorted to changing Harry to kidnap Rosannah."

"Harry? I know Reggie promised him he would change him but there was no way on this Earth he would have ever actually changed him. Now I know that you're definitely lying," she scoffs.

"It looks like there are some things that Regius kept, even from you. Let me enlighten you. When Alex failed for the third time, Regius resorted to turning Harry into a vampire and while he had Alex send me and Lawrence on a wild goose chase, Harry kidnapped Rosannah. Regius may have originally planned to kill Rosannah, but he changed her instead," I say.

"Seriously, is that the same rubbish you've told Mathias?" She asks.

"Regius told him himself!" I yell.

"He wouldn't do that!" She yells back.

"He would if he thought he could kill Mathias!" I yell.

"That doesn't make any sense!" she screams at me.

"Reggie really hasn't told you? That's some partner you have there!" Rosannah says as she crosses her arms.

"I have had enough of this. I'm going to call him to find out what is going on." Bernadette gets her phone out and calls Regius. The stupid fool isn't answering his mobile, I've tried the idiot three times! I'll have to call his home number," she says with frustration.

"Hello?" answers his widow after three rings.

"Is Reggie there?" asks Bernadette in a calm and polite voice.

"No he's not. He hasn't been home for a while. When you find him can you tell him to get his ass home please!" she says and hangs up.

"This is great. He's gone AWOL!" Bernadette says with frustration.

"Let me put you out of your misery and tell you, because I can guarantee that Regius will not be giving you any answers. Mathias is over seven thousand years old. He was the first vampire but he was destructible. He spent some time creating indestructible vampires. Once he managed it he disappeared, changed his skin and body parts, and then re-appeared. He has kept it a secret all these years. Only Mathias and I knew about this," I explain.

"Destructible?" she asks confused.

"Yes."

"That doesn't explain why Reggie would try to kill him though."

"I may have said about Mathias's indiscretion while unbeknownst to me, Regius was within ear shot. Fuelled with this information he then got Harry to come and kill Mathias. When that failed he came himself to finish the task. Because he thought he would be able to kill Mathias he revealed everything to us, including your involvement in certain things and why he wanted to kill Mathias. He hoped that with Mathias dead and with no successor picked, The Synod would dissolve."

"So Mathias can be killed? Interesting," she says with a sly smile.

"Not anymore. I have managed to change him into one of us. I have been telling him for years I should try to change him," I say.

"Oh wait now it all makes sense. We had all wondered why Mathias would pander to you. We all knew you had some kind of hold over him, but we didn't know what. That was it wasn't it?" she asks.

"Yes, it was," I confirm.

"Now you have no hold over him at all. That was a bit stupid wasn't it?" She asks.

"I did not do it to get my own way if that is what you are suggesting. It seems that some of my words have fallen on deaf ears. Like I have already told you, I tried to convince Mathias for years."

"After yours and Reggie's betrayal, I doubt that Mathias will have any trouble listening to Raphael and after all Raphael has done for Mathias, I'm sure he will still have the same if not more pull than he had before," says Rosannah.

"Mathias will get over it," Bernadette says, dismissing Rosannah with a hand.

"No he will not and neither will I. I know that you are the other monster who tormented and killed me and my family that day," I say.

"Yeah, so what?" She says.

"Why did you do it?" I ask her.

"I'm a vampire." She laughs.

"That excuse will only hold up for so long before it becomes a joke," says Rosannah.

"You're trying to tell me about being a vampire when you've only been one for five minutes? Don't make me laugh!" she yells at Rosannah.

"In that *five minutes* she has proven that she is a way better and nobler vampire than you have ever been! Now tell me why you *really* murdered and changed my family," I demand.

"I was bored. I went along with it because it was fun. Reggie did you a huge a favour, look at what you've been able to do and achieve. You and your siblings would have been nothing if it wasn't for us!" She yells and steps towards me. In pure anger I reach out and grab her arms.

"Get the fuck off of me!" she yells with seething anger. With a quick tug her arms come clean off. Bernadette screams once she realises what has happened.

"You ripped my arms off! How the fuck did you manage to do that?!" she screams in horror. Rosannah steps forward.

"When Reggie turned me into a vampire he made a huge mistake. You see, I am able to kill vampires and after the success of Raphael turning Mathias, I attempted to turn Raphael. We weren't too sure if it had fully worked, but now we know it has," Rosannah says with a smile.

"Regius did not make a mistake. There needs to be a way to deal with vile creatures like you," I say to Bernadette while correcting Rosannah.

"Why don't you go after Reggie; he was the one who changed your precious Rosannah!" she says.

"How do you think we found out about Rosannah's ability to kill our kind?" I ask her calmly while using the hand end of one of her detached arms to point at her.

"What?!" she cries.

"It's true, I killed Reggie, but Raphael, we discovered my ability when I killed Harry," Rosannah points out.

"Ah yes. You are right," I say thoughtfully.

"You've killed *two* of us?" Bernadette yelps.

"Oh yes, and I don't plan to stop there. There will always be naughty vampires who need to lose their heads." Rosannah laughs as I drop Bernadette's arms. With that Bernadette goes to take off.

CHAPTER TWENTY-FOUR

Rosannah

As Bernadette goes to flee Raphael reaches out and grabs her by her shoulders. Flinging her around, he pushes her onto the floor. Her screams of pure terror go straight through me. Raphael grabs one leg and rips it off. It's followed by wails and howls. He then grabs the other and repeats.

"This is for me, my family, and Rosannah," he shouts as he takes her head in his hands. With a guttural roar from Raphael and a high pitched screech from Bernadette, Raphael twists her head clean off. He drops her head and he crumples to the floor. I race over and take him in my arms.

"I am sorry. I did not think this would hit me as hard as it has. I have dreamed of the moment I could avenge my family all this time and you have made it possible."

I cradle him against me as sobs wrack through him. After a while he pulls back from me with a look of sorrow. "Let us put her with the others and update Mathias."

"Are you sure you're okay to do this yet?" I ask gently.

"Yes, I am fine." He smiles softly at me.

I gather up Bernadette and we race off back to Raphael's crypt. He takes her body and opens a coffin.

"Who's that?" I ask with my nose wrinkled up.

"My cousin Ludwig," he says with a grim expression. Once the Coffin is sealed we head back to the house and Raphael calls Mathias.

"Raphael," Mathias answers.

"Bernadette has been dealt with. She admitted everything," Raphael says.

"Two traitors, I can't believe it. Thank you Raphael," he says.

"You do not need to thank me," Raphael says, dismissing Mathias sentiment.

"I do so thank you again, for everything."

"Oh well, I…" Raphael stammers.

"What Raphael means to say is you're welcome," I say down the line.

"I owe you big time Raphael," Mathias says.

"No you do not. Forget about it and enjoy your evening. We will inform Porticus and Vladimir when you are ready," Raphael says and hangs up.

"Raphael, what was that all about?" I ask, questioning him cutting the call dead.

"I do not handle some things very well," he admits.

"I can see that," I say and press a kiss to his lips. My handsome vampire boyfriend grows more human every day.

CHAPTER TWENTY-FIVE

Brianna

Finishing work is my favourite time of the working day. I look forward to getting home, cooking dinner, and spending time with the love of my life, Michael. Today is definitely no exception. With Rosannah away on holiday, my work load has doubled and I have to deal with Paul mainly by myself. I can't get out of the office any quicker. I get home, put dinner on, have a shower, and just as I'm serving up, Michael arrives home from work. He's a building site manager. He was quite secretive about his line of work for some time. I did get suspicious until he took me to a works drinks night where I met his co-workers and boss.

"Just in time, like always." I smile. Michael goes and freshens himself up and joins me on the couch for dinner. "One day we'll make room for a dinner table," I joke. Michael doesn't do his normal chuckle. Instead he looks at his food with serious consternation. "Is everything okay?" I ask him. Worry crosses his features as he clears his throat. "Is dinner that much of a disappointment?"

"It's not the dinner," he says quietly.

"So there is a problem," I state.

"It depends on what you consider a problem. I don't see it as a problem but you might," Michael says, turning to me.

"What kind of *problem* is it?" I ask, worry building up inside of me. Michael puts his dinner in the kitchen and comes and sits back down next to me.

"You may want to put your dinner down and break out the wine," he suggests.

"Am I really going to need it?" I ask.

"I think so," he says. Against my gut reaction I do as Michael suggests. Once I have a glass of wine I sit back down. Michael goes to say something numerous times but stops himself every time.

"Can you please just say *something*?" I ask.

"You know that I love you and I want to be with you, right?" he asks. This is what guys say when they've had enough of you. It'll be the *it's not you it's me* next.

"You're breaking up with me aren't you? I can't believe it!" I say getting up and nearly spilling my wine.

"No, no. That's not it! I want to be with you and I don't want to lose you. Sit down," he pleads.

"Why would you be afraid to lose me? What have you done?" I ask nervously.

"Look, there are some things about me I haven't told you. There not the kind of things that can just be told. They have implications."

"You're gay aren't you?" I say.

"No, I'm not gay!" he says and with unbelievable speed, he is by the window. He turns to look at me. "I'm a vampire."

My mind is bombarded by what I have just seen and I slowly sit back down.

"I know there's rumours about the Monstrum house, but I mean come on! Vampires don't really exist."

"That's my brother's house. My two brothers, sister and I are all vampires. We really do exist," he says.

"Absolutely no way!" I say standing back up.

"I can prove it."

"Go on then." I demand. In a split second he is in front of me with fangs on display and pitch black eyes. "Party tricks!" I yell. Michael races off and produces a knife on his return. He stabs at his arm with it and I scream. Expecting blood, I cover my face.

"Look at me!" Michael demands.

"No, there's going to be blood everywhere!" I scream.

"There's no blood. You have to trust me," he says with a calm and hushed tone. Reluctantly I open my eyes and see the knife is against his skin with no blood. He then starts to stab his arm repeatedly gradually with increasing in speed.

"Stop, stop!" I yell. He stops and looks at me.

"There's only one thing that can break vampire skin and those are these," he says and his fangs are back on display.

"So, you really are a vampire?" I ask.

"Yes, I really am." I watch as his eyes fade to a light grey.

"Your eyes..."

"These are natural vampire eyes."

I am now full of questions.

"So when you said your brothers and sister were vampires does that mean you can breed? Oh God could I be pregnant with vampire babies?!" I ask.

"No, we can't breed. We have to be changed." He explains and goes to sit on the couch.

"You were all changed? How does that even happen?" I ask with raised eyebrows.

"It was against our will but it's a long story, there are more important things I need to tell you," he says and pats the seat next to him.

"There's more?" I ask as I sit next to him.

"I wish there wasn't, but there is," he says with a frown.

"Like what? Surely it can't be worse."

"As I said, my brother, the eldest one, he owns the *Monstrum house* as you call it. His name is Raphael and he is your best friend's boyfriend," he says. It takes a second for me to process that information.

"Wait what? Raphael is a vampire? The owner of the Monstrum house? The one who's going out with my best friend. I told Rosannah about the rumours!" I say.

"The rumours are true," he says calmly.

"And my own best friend didn't tell me a thing!" I say with a huff.

"In all fairness to Rosannah, she wasn't actually allowed to tell humans. We vampires have the ability to make humans forget things, but it wouldn't work on Rosannah. We kept her hostage because of it."

"Hostage?" I ask.

"Yes, we couldn't have her telling anyone about us. We have a council called The Synod. They collectively agreed to keep Rosannah as a hostage until she either died or got changed into one of us, but it backfired on us because after a week we all had a falling out and Raphael threw her out of his home because he thought it would be safer for her. He then realised he couldn't be without her and went and got her back. The Synod agreed to allow this arrangement except for one member, he was against everything and took it upon himself to kidnap Rosannah and changed her into a vampire against her will."

"Rosannah is a vampire?" I ask.

"Yes, she is, and she's adapted beautifully." He smiles.

"This is so crazy! My best friend is not only dating a vampire but is now one herself! Have you actually made me forget stuff?" I ask suspiciously.

"Yes I have," he admits.

"Can you make me remember it all?" I ask. Do I really want to know? Yes, I think I do.

"I can, but let me tell you some things first before I do okay?"

"Okay"

"Know that I now love you with all of my heart and that I want to be with you more than anything in this world."

"Okay" I reply. Michael gets down to my level and stares me in the eyes. Soon memories start to swirl back into my mind. There are too many to comprehend. They are all horrible and hideous. "You're a monster!" I yell and back up from him. "How do I know that you are telling the truth? That you still don't want Rosannah and this is all a ploy?"

"I knew you'd be upset" he says.

"Upset?! I'm a little more than *upset!*"

"There's only one way for you to know I'm telling the truth. Speak to Rosannah. She will tell you the truth. Also know that Rosannah has the ability to quite literally rip my head off," he says with a shiver.

"Can't all vampires do that?" I ask.

"No. We were completely indestructible and then Rosannah came along. She has the ability to kill us. Look, I'll go out so you can talk to Rosannah. Give me a call when you're ready to see me again. I hope you will be," he says as he kisses my forehead.

"But isn't she meant to be on holiday?" I ask.

"No, she's at Raphael's. It's just a cover story because we can't go telling everyone what's really happened," he says and then he's gone. I sigh in exasperation, pick up my phone, and call Rosannah.

"Hi," she says.

"We need to talk." I say.

"He told you didn't he?" she asks.

"Oh he told me alright."

"I'll be there in two minutes," she says and hangs up. Two minutes later she knocks at the door. I open it to reveal my best friend with light grey eyes and pale skin.

CHAPTER TWENTY-SIX

Rosannah

Arriving at Brianna's, I have no idea what to expect. What I get is a relatively calm Brianna. She lets me in and I take a seat on the couch.

"You have been seriously holding out on me," she says.

"I had to. Goodness knows what would have happened to me and they would have wiped your memory anyway. You would never have known I'd existed."

"Well, I was made to forget a lot of things," she says.

"What do you mean by *was*?" I ask.

"He made me remember everything." She says.

"He *made* you?" I ask with raised eyebrows.

"Yes, no, I mean I asked him to,"she says. A flood of relief flows through me. I thought I was going to have to rip hisdick off.

"I know that some of the things aren't very nice but he really does love you now," I say with a smile.

"All of the stuff he had me forget *wasn't* very nice! How am I supposed to get over it all? How can he even love me after treating me like that?" She asks.

"I know that. He had me fooled. I was suspicious at first,"

"You kept calling him Nicholas and I got so angry at you, I'm so sorry," she says.

"It's okay Brianna. He changed my mind and had me convinced until Raphael came to our double date. He knew straight away that Michael was Nicholas. He had you so brainwashed that there was nothing we could actually do. Fortunately, Nicholas saw sense. He asked me about telling you about everything. He wanted to be truthful with you. Have a proper relationship with you that wasn't based on lies. Yes, what he did wasn't good at all, but can you look past it? Raphael had intended to use me and abuse me. Heck, he even did to a point. I managed to deal with it because I knew it was part of his nature. He's a three-hundred-year old vampire who became jaded over time. He lost his way and his regard for life, but our love saved him, brought him back to the world of the living. It will never excuse the things he has done in the past, but it makes up for the here and now. That is what Nicholas wants with you. To start afresh and be a creature that is worth something."

"I suppose when you put it like that it's not too bad. It's just such a shock. The whole beginning of our relationship, the fact he and his siblings are vampires, that you're a vampire. Oh wait a minute! When you had lost your virginity and you couldn't tell me why, I thought that you were having an affair with a married man or with a woman! This is why you couldn't tell me wasn't it? The reason was because Raphael was a vampire!" she exclaims.

"That's right. I also had get on with life after everyone had their memories wiped so that they didn't know I had been to his house to do the evaluation," I say.

"The valuation never happened,"she says.

"Exactly, you and everyone else were made to forget," I explain.

"Michael, I mean Nicholas, was meant to have made me remember everything!" she yells.

"It was Raphael who made you forget. Nicholas can't make you remember things other vampires have made you forget. It works with instructions but not memories," I say.

"Instructions?" she asks confused.

"Yes. When we were on our double date Nicholas instructed you to go to the ladies so he and Raphael could discuss the situation. I came to get you, but you wouldn't come back until I told you that Michael had asked you to come back."

"You see how messed up this is?" she asks.

"I do get that, more than you could ever know, but he's trustworthy, he just got a little crazy jealous that his brother had something he didn't. He didn't even really want me, he just thought he did."

"Really? I mean *really,* really?" she asks.

"Yes. So, what are you going to do about all of this? Nicholas really does love you and wants to be with you."

"Is it true that you can kill him?" she asks.

"Yes, it's true."

"And you've forgiven him?"

"Yes I have. We all have our crazy moments, but don't forgive him just because I have."

"I'll forgive him, but it's not because you have. I'm not a sheep. It takes brainwashing to get me to mindlessly follow." She laughs. I suppose it's a good thing she can see a funny side to all of this. "It's because I love him and I can see how much it must

146

mean to him to tell me the truth. Maybe I'm crazy but I see real bravery in that."

"I'm glad to hear it. I best get going then, you have some more talking to do," I say and head over to the front door.

"Rosannah?"

"Yes?" I reply.

"Does this mean that you are leaving Tilberry Sales?" she asks.

"No, not yet. I should let you know that I've moved into Raphael's too."

"What? You have held out so much on me!"

"I know, I know. I really am sorry about that, but you must be aware that now you know all of this you cannot tell a soul. If you do your memory will be wiped as well as anyone you have told. The secrecy of vampires is at stake."

"I won't tell anyone!" she says.

"I know you won't, but what kind of friend would I be if I didn't tell you something incredibly important about vampires when I can. I'm so glad you know about all of this now. I don't need to hide or lie about things anymore," I say.

"Me too." She smiles. I Leave her apartment and as I'm walking down the stairs I hear her call Nicholas. A few minutes later I see him heading towards me and stop.

"Is she okay?" he asks.

"Yes, she's fine. I don't have to rip your head off," I joke. "Look, I think it's best we keep the fact that Brianna knows all of this between me, you, Raphael and Lawrence. I know The Synod is a little broken, but we don't really want or need Brianna to be a hostage or have it ordered that she must be made to forget when she's actually okay with all of this."

"I completely agree. Evangeline has a very big mouth, but I will tell Lawrence the next time I see him. Thank you Rosannah." He smiles and with that he races off and I race home.

When I arrive I head into the TV room to find Raphael watching Sherlock with Marmalade on his lap.

"How did it go?" he asks as he strokes behind her ears. Marmalade purrs in appreciation. I'm amazed at how well she's settling in, but I don't know how Raphael is settling in with Marmalade.

"I will tell you after I've fed Marmalade."

"I have already done that," he says. I don't mean to but I pull a face. "I looked up on the internet about looking after cats. Do not worry, I will not let her starve nor will I let her toilet box overflow," he says while looking at Marmalade. I'm quite surprised. It looks like Raphael has really taken to my cat, well now she's our cat I guess.

"Okay, the talk with Brianna went badly to begin with. It was a lot for her to take in, what with him telling her certain things and then making her remember everything," I say.

"He did that?" he asks incredulously.

"She asked him to. It saved explaining everything," I say shrugging my shoulders.

"I get that. I am quite proud of my brother and I do hope they make it through this. It cannot be easy for her,"he says thoughtfully. I smile at his words.

"I know, but I will be there for her if she needs me," I say.

"I will be there too as well, for Nicholas," he says. It's nice to know that Raphael has forgiven Nicholas. I smile to myself and go sit down next to Raphael. We snuggle with Marmalade and watch the rest of Sherlock.

CHAPTER TWENTY-SEVEN

Raphael

The following morning, I head to the kitchen for some breakfast blood. Rosannah soon joins me.

"Do you really think Brianna and Nicholas will be okay?" I ask her. I really hope they will be. I am now happy to completely forgive my brother. I may treat my siblings with contempt, but I do genuinely care for them. I would never tell them this, I would not hear the end of it.

"Yes I do. They spent last night having lots of hot sex,"she says with a smile. I pull a face and Rosannah laughs.

"How do you know that?" I ask with raised eyebrows.

"If she wasn't then they would of had a fight and she would have called me. No word means they had make up sex all night long."

I hear the front door open and close and Evangeline appears in the kitchen.

"Hey, where is everyone?" she asks.

"The twins are at their own homes," I reply.

"That's not what I meant,"she says with a pout.

"Who else could you possibly mean?" I ask perplexed.

"Something very weird is going on," she says, ignoring my question.

"The only strange thing here is you," I say deadpan.

"Raphael!" Rosannah chastises me.

"Forgive me Evangeline. Continue," I say.

"I have contacted Mathias to get an update on things and he has refused to tell me anything. I then contacted the other members of The Synod and two are missing. No one will tell me anything and I don't understand what's going on," she says.

"You do realise that you are *not* apart of The Synod and they have no reason to tell you anything," I say.

"But they have before," she whines.

"But they are not obliged to, so if they refuse you should just accept that," I say.

"You can tell me though," she pleads. With everything that has happened we could not risk telling Evangeline and have critical information leaked. I am the reason why The Synod have not told her anything. There is no reason to keep anything from her now.

"A lot has happened and because we did not want anything leaked we did not tell you," I state.

"But you can trust me!" she whines.

"I know you are trustworthy, but you accidently let things slip and we could not allow that to happen," I say soothingly.

"Well, are you going to tell me what's been happening or just keep waffling at me?" she asks. Anger rises in me, but I push it back down.

"Well you already know that Regius kidnapped and changed Rosannah. What you do not know is that Mathias was destructible."

"Destructible? What does that mean?" She asks with her head tilted to the side. It looks like I may have to *dumb this down* for her. How could I not realise this?

"He could be killed."

"That's ridiculous! No vampire can be killed!"

"Mathias could because he was a different type of vampire. He was the first vampire. He developed the indestructible vampire."

"That makes no sense whatsoever. You're making this up!" This is just like Bernadette all over again. Vampires are so sure of the way things are, it is how it has always been. No vampire apart Mathias and myself knew that a vampire that could be killed existed.

"Just take my word for it. Regius had changed Harry into a vampire to help him kidnap Rosannah. I let slip that Mathias could be killed and Regius had Harry come to kill him."

"Harry is a vampire? Mathias isn't dead, I spoke to him not that long ago," she says narrowing her eyes at me and placing her hands on her hips. I let an involuntary growl escape.

"Was. Harry was a vampire," I grate.

"How can he not be a vampire anymore?" she asks suspiciously.

"Because Rosannah killed him."

"Was he like Mathias too?"

"No, Mathias was the only one of his kind. He made sure any others like himself were wiped out."

"So Rosannah killed a vampire like us?"

"Yes, she did. Then I changed Mathias to be like us, me and you, to protect him."

"I don't understand," she says.

"That is because you keep asking stupid questions!" I yell.

"Raphael," Rosannah says to try and calm me down. I steady myself and try again.

"I will only explain this once. Do *not* interrupt me, okay?" I ask. Evangeline nods her head. "Like I said, Regius overheard me say Mathias could be killed. He sent Harry, who he had been turned into a vampire to kidnap Rosannah, to kill Rosannah. It was then that we discovered Rosannah capabilities."

"There's no way she could have killed a vampire," she says pointing to Rosannah.

"We have bodies to prove it," I say.

"Bodies?" she asks horrified.

"Yes. Myself, Mathias, Lawrence, and Nicholas witnessed Rosannah kill Harry. After the incident, I put Harry's body into a coffin in the crypt. We kept it to ourselves because we did not want the news getting to Regius. Once Mathias was made into a vampire like us, he stayed with Nicholas and Lawrence at Lawrence's house. We knew Regius would turn up at some point. When he did, Rosannah killed him. His body was then put in another coffin in the crypt," I say grimly.

"Reggie is dead?" she asks with a sadness in her eyes. Of course she would be sad that Regius is dead, she does not understand what he has done.

"Yes. It is nothing less than what he deserved. Rosannah then made me like her, so now I can kill vampires as well."

"You can kill us too? How do you know you can kill us?"

"Because I have killed a vampire," I state.

"Who?" She asks with a blank expression.

"In a bid to stop Rosannah from finishing him off, Regiustold us that Bernadette was working with him. So we went to see her and I killed her," I say.

"They're both dead? You both killed them? Impossible," she states.

"Go to the crypt and look in uncle Frederick, great uncle Julian, and cousin Ludwig's coffins. You will see all the evidence that you need," I say.

She races off. After ten minutes she has not come back and I begin to worry. Maybe this is too much for her. Just as I am about to go and see where she may have got to we hear an almighty bang. Dashing out to the hall way we see that the front door has been swung open so hard that it has been destroyed. When the dust settles we see a very distressed Evangeline. She really has not taken this very well.

"Are you okay Evangeline?" asks a concerned Rosannah.

"Don't you dare talk to me," she grits out at her. Rosannah gasps. "You," Evangeline points to me. "You have no idea what you've done."

"What are you talking about?" I ask.

"You both actually killed Reggie and Bernadette!" She yells.

"Those two are the reason our family is dead and we are vampires!" I explain.

"Of course they were!" she yells throwing her arms up in the air. "Everything was planned out. Everything was meant to be perfect. The plan was perfect!" she sobs.

"What was perfect? What plan are you talking about?" I ask.

"Oh, open your eyes Raphael! Oh it's too hard for you to do while you're so wrapped up in *her*!" she says pointing at Rosannah. I am beyond confused. What has gotten into my sister!

"I really have no idea what you are talking about."

"Surely you know about Granddad's obsession with vampires?" she asks.

"I knew he had an interest, but I would not have called it an obsession," I say.

"Oh it was an obsession alright. He used to spend hours telling me about them. Because I was the only one who actually believed him when he told me all about them. It wasn't long before I became just as obsessed. One day he told me he was sure he had seen real vampires. It was his dream to become one so I asked him if he was going to ask to be changed. You want to know what he said? The fool said no! He explained that if they really were vampires, they were too dangerous to approach. The stupid old man dreamt all his life of becoming a vampire, but was too scared to do anything about it when the opportunity hit him in his big idiotic face!" she says. I look at Rosannah who looks horrified.

"Okay, so our grandfather was more into vampires than I thought, but I do not understand what this has to do with anything."

"You wouldn't, would you? How would you?" She asks to thin air. "Because granddad was too scared to do anything, I took matters into my own hands."

"Took them into your own hands?" I ask. I now understand why Rosannah looks so damn shocked.

"Yes. I approached the vampires. They were Reggie and Bernadette. I told them that I knew what they were and threatened them to make me one of them or I would tell everyone. They obviously found that hilarious, but when I explained that I had hidden diary entries around that would be found eventually containing condemning information about them, they stopped laughing. I was completely bluffing, ofcourse, butI wasn't going to let them know that. While they were undecided I told them they didn't have the guts to change me. That was the decider and we struck up a deal at that moment." She smiles. My stomach sinks as I realise where this is going.

"What kind of deal?" I ask quietly.

"Yours and my immortality in exchange for the others' lives." She says. I am glad I am not a human, because I am sure I would have thrown up by now.

"You are the reason that our family was murdered and we were changed?!" I ask incredulously.

"Yes, although the twins weren't supposed to survive, those two annoying idiots were supposed to die with the rest of them," she says angrily. How could she think of our brothers, our *family,* like this?!

"You do know that Regius and Bernadette had planned to betray you and kill us too?" I ask.

"Yes, I was quite annoyed at that, but what did I really expect from vampires? I'm just happy I got part of what I had wanted"

"What about what the rest of us wanted?" I ask.

"Like that mattered." She laughs. I stare at the stranger in front of me. Everything about her different. The way she talks, the way she behaves, even carries herself has changed. Gone is the bumbling, half-witted sister and in her place is a sinister, evil creature that I do not recognise.

Vampires can be quite evil, but when it comes to any kind of family, whether blood related or not, we still have morals and standards.

CHAPTER TWENTY-EIGHT

Rosannah

I am sick to my stomach by what I am hearing. This is *Evangeline*. Silly, soppy, loveable Evangeline. What the hell happened to her? Where did she go?

"I spent years acting like the idiot, I couldn't have any of you suspect athing. It was pure torture, I had to put up with you and the twins treating me like a piece of dirt. I forgave you, but those two I hated. Once you had the ability to eject vampires into space, I did everything I could to get them set up for crimes so they could be got rid of, but having to play dumb meant I wasn't very successful," she says with a huff.

"Why on Earth would you do any of this?" Raphael asks in a small voice. God, what must be going through his head hearing all of this?

"It was supposed to be me and you. Just us," she says with forlorn. Something doesn't feel right how she looks and what she just said. It's almost as if she has some kind of *feelings* for him.

"Why just us?" Raphael asks suspiciously. Does he really want the answer!

"Why this, why that!" Evangeline yells.

"You are not making much sense so forgive me if I seem a little confused and heaven forbid I ask any questions!" He yells. Evangeline is taken aback a little but she recovers.

"I have been in love with you for years. We were meant to be together forever!" She sobs.

That has to be the most disgusting thing I have *ever* heard!

"You have got to be kidding me! You are my sister! We are blood related!" Yells Raphael.

"Oh Raphael, you utter fool! Mummy and daddy never told you their dirty secret did they? I was adopted!" she says.

"That is not true!"

"It is! After the moron twins ruined mummy dear's body, she couldn't have any more children. They were so desperate for a girl that they adopted me. They never planned to even tell me the truth but granddad did. Granddad would tell me everything. Shame he was such a wimp and he had to die in the end. So you see, I'm not actually related to you!" She says. I am so shocked and disturbed that I keep my mouth clamped shut.

"And you think that makes all of this okay?" Raphael asks with raised eyebrows.

"It *was* all okay. I laid in wait until the perfect moment. That moment never happened because *she* turned up and ruined everything," She says pointing at me with a look of pure hatred. "When Rosannah first came on the scene I wasn't too worried. I thought you were going to do your normal thing and that soon she would be broken and discarded like so many others in the past, but you just had to go and reveal yourself to her didn't you?" She says and turns to me. "You couldn't just be made to forget could you?" she asks me.

"It's not my fault," I blurt out unable to control my reaction.

"It's your fault, it's *all your fault*!" she says. "That is what drew him to you. You were a new kind of challenge, especially with the hard to get I'm a virgin thing you had going on! Telling him you were a virgin was the worst thing you could have done!" she says. "You want to know why Reggie was after you? Because I *told* him to!"

"What?" I ask incredulously.

"That's right. I tried all sorts of things. The first thing was to get The Synod involved. I thought they'd take you away. You were a huge liability to them but to my horror only Reggie and Porticus voiced their concerns. There was no way Porticus would team up with me, but I knew Reggie and Bernadette would. We had made numerous deals in the past and I knew they would gladly work with me on this. I got Reggie to brain wash Alex. I knew he would be the perfect candidate to use. I had met him at party of Cindy's. She'd tried to set us up but he really wasn't my type. I prefer my men without a pulse," she says. I feel so sick listening to her talking. She got poor Alex involved in all of this?

"So were you one of the vampires that spoke to Alex on the phone?" Asks Raphael.

"No, that was Reggie and Bernadette. It unfortunately didn't work out how I wanted, so it was a miracle when what's his face, Nicholas, showed signs that he may like Rosannah. Some manipulation and pushes in the right direction and he thought he was in love. He was so easy to convince that it was the best thing to challenge you. That day couldn't have gone any better! And then when you wiped any trace of yourself from Rosannah's life,it was just brilliant!" She exclaims.

"But that wasn't enough for you was it?" Asks Raphael.

"No it wasn't, and it would have ended there if you could have left Rosannah alone when you threw her out, but you couldn't, could you?" She asks Raphael. "I had to get Alex involved again. I hoped that if Rosannah fell for him she'd forget all about you and I wouldn't have to have her killed, but you just had to get involved again, having that other twat keep an eye on Alex and before I knew it you were back together! I must admit, I had no idea that what's his face had come back and gone all brainwashing happy on Rosannah's best friend. If I had known, I would have played that game too."

"So you were willing to have Rosannah killed?" Raphael asks through gritted teeth.

"Oh, I tried on numerous times to off her" she says as if it's nothing. I gasp. "I don't know what you're so upset about. You're here aren't you? Forever unfortunately. I tried as hard as I could to end you the second time around, but with Raphael following you around like a love sick puppy, I stood no chance!"

"You want to know why you never stood a chance at actually succeeding?" I ask her. She grins cynically at me. "Because we were destined to be together and our love is stronger than anything this world has ever known and nobody, including your insane ass, is every going to break that or us!" I say. Her smile falters but returns as she focuses on Raphael.

"So *brother,* what are you going to do now? Lock me up? *Kill* me?" she asks tilting her head to the side like she used to.

"I have no idea,"he admits. Raphael must be completely torn and jumbled up inside. I feel so devastated for him and my heart aches for him.

"Ah, so you are going to let The Synod decide? I think you will struggle with them. They have a problem with doing anything the *right* way," she says. Raphael turns and gives me a questioning look. He looks so lost and confused. While we are looking at each other, Evangeline takes the opportunity to run off. I go to chase her but Raphael stops me.

"No, let her go,"he says, defeated.

"What?" I ask.

"I cannot act on what I have heard without speaking to my family first."

I read between the lines. He needs support after this and I get that.

"Okay, let's head over to Lawrence's," I say and hand in hand we head over to his.

CHAPTER TWENTY-NINE

Raphael

On our way I pull out my phone and dial Nicholas. "Raph?" he answers.

"You must come to Lawrence's immediately," I say and hang up.

We all arrive at Lawrence's within minutes.

"Oh, something really bad must have happened. You look more dead than usual," says Lawrence when he lets us all in. I glare at him, but start to explain.

"I have something rather disturbing to tell you and I think it best you both took a seat," I say. Worry flashes across my brothers faces, but the concern is gone as they take a seat in Lawrence's front room. "Rosannah and I had thought that now Regius and Bernadette were dead everything was over but we were very wrong."

"So that bitch is dead? Way to Rosannah!" says Lawrence he goes to high five her, but I stop him.

"Rosannah did not kill her, I did," I admit.

"Woah Raph! So you let Rosannah get her teeth into you!" Lawrence laughs.

"Something like that, but that is not important right now. There has been someone else who has been involved with Regius and Bernadette. They are the main figure in all of this. They were the one who had our family murdered, were responsible for us being changed and everything that has happened to Rosannah," I say.

"Who? I will see that they are made to pay for this!" Yells Lawrence.

"It is not as easy as that.".

"How? Whoever it is needs to be punished!" Yells Nicholas.

"I agree but this is very difficult," I try to reason.

"Just tell us who for goodness sake Raph," pleads Lawrence.

"Evangeline," I say with regret.

"What?" says Lawrence.

"No way," says Nicholas. I wish I were lying, I truly wish it was not true, but it is and is made even worse that she did this all just to get me.

"Yes, brothers. Our sister has betrayed us; she has always betrayed us. She made a deal with Regius and Bernadette to turn her and myself into vampires while the rest of you were killed. Regius had planned to kill us all but changed his mind. It was also Evangeline who was behind the whole Alex plan. She wanted to remove Rosannah from the picture and in the end had Regius agree to kill Rosannah, but we know he changed the plan once again. This is why she kept telling The Synod things, she wanted them to remove Rosannah. She even manipulated Nicholas to think he was in love with Rosannah and to act upon it," I say regretfully. Nicholas looks almost broken but Lawrence looks pretty angry.

"You told Evangeline, but not me?" he asks.

"I didn't tell her anything, but she did say some odd things to me,"he says.

"Like what?" I ask.

"She told me that I needed to seize the day. Kept talking to me about love, telling me the signs of being in love and that I shouldn't let it pass me by, even if the object of anyone's affections belonged to someone else. That love was worth fighting for,"he says shrugging his shoulders.

"And you never thought to tell anyone about this?" asks Lawrence.

"I thought it was odd, but I didn't think for one second my sister was plotting against us all!" Nicholas yells.

"That's fair enough," Rosannah says.

"Why on Earth would she do any of this?" asks Nicholas. "Why would she do that to me or any of us? It just doesn't make sense."

"She is in love with me and it was all part of her plan to get me" I admit, feeling absolutely sick to my stomach.

"Urgh! That's vile!" says Lawrence.

"I second that!" says Nicholas with disgust.

"She said she was adopted. I do not know how true that actually is. I do plan to research her claim," I say. I can access any records I want in any part of the world. If it exists, I can get to it.

"Even if it's true it doesn't make it anywhere near right!" says Lawrence.

"I completely agree with you," I say.

"Me too," agrees Rosannah.

"Please tell me her head is ripped off and she's hidden in the family crypt?" says Nicholas through gritted teeth.

"She is not, she used our shock as an opportunity to escape. I wanted to come here and discuss this with you first and then talk to Mathias about it. I also think that we are in the position to tell Vladimir and Porticus. If they are somehow involved, which I doubt, then they too will end up like Regius and Bernadette," I say.

"I doubt it too. Reggie was always funny with you and Bernadette couldn't give two shits about anything but herself. I don't know what the fuck to think about Evangeline, but Vladimir and Porticus have always been great friends of yours and ours. Vladimir even went down the official route to get Cindy changed," says Nicholas.

"We never suspected Evangeline and look what she has done," says Lawrence.

"Well now that you two can kill vampires, any betrayal can be dealt with like you said, but if there isn't any then Mathias, Vladimir and Porticus, will vote you kill Evangeline. I am perfectly happy with that. She is no sister of mine!" says Nicholas.

"I agree," says Lawrence.

"I am torn." I admit.

"How can you possibly be torn?" asks Lawrence.

"You are not the one she is in love with. None of this is your fault!" I say.

"None of this is your fault either!" yells Rosannah.

"Maybe, but I cannot help but feel guilty." I say.

"I know Raph," says Lawrence softly. "Hopefully we will all get over all this betrayal to some extent, but I think it's time to tell what's left of The Synod," he says.

"Before I go, I must ask one more thing. I have an incestuous sister and a psycho brother, no offense," I say.

"None taken," says Nicholas.

"Have you got anything to get off your chest? Now would be the time to speak up," I say, pointing at Lawrence.

"No, I'm good," he says holding his palms up at me.

"I know I have done some very questionable things in the past but surely I do not deserve to be the reason for all of this madness?" I ask.

"Well, what you deserve is debatable," says Lawrence with a grin.

"Lawrence! You're not helping!" chastises Rosannah.

"Just trying to crack a joke," he says bashfully.

"Well it's not funny!" says Rosannah.

"Look, this needs sorting out," says Nicholas.

"You are right. I will go and discuss this with the Synod," I say.

"If you do decide not to tell them,I would be down for that. Go find Evangeline and sort her out ourselves," says Nicholas.

"I am certain they should now know. I just thought it was more respectful to tell you first," I say.

"Oh bless, he respects us. That's touched my heart," says Lawrence.

"Sarcastic creep," I mutter.

"Wow, that didn't last long." Lawrencelaughs

"Two seconds? That's still a record though," Nicholas adds.

"Yep, that may be true, but he undone the love with the insult. That's not cool," says Lawrence.

"You have no idea what cool even means," I say.

"He's back to hating us," says Nicholas.

"I am going home to talk with The Synod," I say deadpan.

"That's it, run from your feelings. You'll always be emotionally stunted," Lawrence says with mock seriousness as I walk off taking Rosannah by the hand.

"I have lost most of my family; do I really want to be left with those two?" I ask her as we leave.

"Ow brother!" yells Lawrence and Nicholas.

Rosannah and I race back to our home and Rosannah is laughing when we get there.

"Why are you laughing?" I ask her.

"The relationship you have with your brothers is adorable." She smiles.

"Adorable? They are both the most annoying creatures on the planet!" I say as I make my way to the dining room.

"That may be true but you love them so much, it's easy to see," Rosannah says with a smile and follows me.

"Do not tell them that, ever," I say and she smiles knowingly at me. I take out my phone and send a text to Mathias. He arrives within minutes.

"What happened to your front door?" he asks, joining us in the dining room.

"Evangeline happened to it," I say. Mathias looks quite confused. I then proceed to tell him everything that has transpired.

"I should have known. The amount of times Evangeline called me shot up dramatically once Rosannah was on the scene and I didn't think anything of it" he admits.

"None of us did. We would never have thought in a million years she was capable of this kind of thing," I say.

"There's no doubt about it, she must be caught and punished, but I have something I must tell you. I am stepping down as leader from The Synod, well stepping away from it all together," he says regretfully.

"You are leaving now?" I ask incredulously.

"I know that now isn't the best time for this."

"That is an understatement," I say.

"I must do what is right for me. It is clear that I wasn't the best at being the leader. Look what happened under my rule. I want you to take my place," he says and claps me on the shoulder.

"You want me to lead?" I ask.

"Yes, we need to talk to Vladimir and Porticus about this and everything," he says.

"Okay, let us get them over here," I say.

With a couple of calls, it is not long before the other two remaining members of The Synod walk in to my dining room.

"I have called you both here because I want to announce to you that I am stepping down and away from The Synod. I am leaving Raphael as my successor. The rules, which were decided some years ago, state that all current members must be present for this of The Synod risks being dissolved. Do you understand and agree with my decision?" he asks.

"I must say, I'm quite surprised you're leaving, but with all that stuff with Regius, I understand and welcome your decisions," says Vladimir.

"I too am surprised, I thought you'd be leader forever, but I respect your choices too," says Porticus.

"Well, I hate to love and leave you all but I have my *retirement* to go and enjoy. If you ever need I am more than happy to help and please don't be strangers," He says, then races off.

"What just happened?" I ask Vladimir.

"You became the leader of The Synod." He smiles.

"The Synod? There are only three of us left. What kind of Synod is that?" I ask. Rosannah looks very thoughtful for a while.

"Why don't you add new members? Your brothers? Even me? What about Cindy and Franklin?" she suggests.

"You would join us?" I ask her.

"Of course I would." She smiles. This woman never fails to amaze me. With everything she has been through she is still so strong and is willing to fight by my side through anything.

"I will go and ask Cindy if she wants to join," says Vladimir.

"I'll check with Franklin too," Porticus says.

"Okay, we will have a meeting in the morning about this," I say.

"Sure, I'll bring Cindy. See you tomorrow," says Vladimir and he races off.

"Same here," nods Porticus and he races off too. Ah, that damn door. I am grateful I have spares. I dash to the garage, pick up a door that is tucked away and in no time at all, it is fitted. Rosannah admires my handy work." There we are, some privacy again," I smile as I take Rosannah in to my arms.

CHAPTER THIRTY
Rosannah

Raphael is quite upset about everything, he's not really showing it, but I know he is. With his arms around me, I can feel the weight of the world on his shoulders.

"I really do not know what to think about all of this," he admits.

"How about we don't think about anything right now," I say and kiss him. He kisses me back and soon it deepens. A growl escapes my throat as I start to moisten. Grabbing him by the collar of his shirt I lead him into the TV room. Making sure Marmalade isn't in the room, I push Raphael on to the couch. He lands with a growl and his eyes turn a dark grey. Kicking off my shoes, I place a foot in his lap for him to spread his knees. I trail my foot from his knee to his crotch and find him rock hard. A moan escapes him as I massage his length with the ball of my foot.

"Rosannah," he moans and I playfully smile at him. Removing my foot, I begin to strip. I start with my sweatshirt slowly riding it up my body. I slide it over my head and then discard it.

"Reow," I hear. I turn to the source of the noise and see my sweatshirt squirming on the floor. Marmalade must have come in as I threw it!

"Oh Marmalade, I'm so sorry," I say and walk over to her to remove my sweatshirt. I pick her up and give her a cuddle and kiss before putting her down. She walks over to Raphael and stares at him.

"What?" he asks her after a short while.

"Reow," she says and carries on staring at him.

"I think she wants her seat back," I laugh.

"Ah, I see. Do forgive me Marmalade," he says and gets up. Marmalade jumps up onto the seat.

"Now, where were we? Ah yes," Raphael says and picks me up. He dashes upstairs and lays down sideways on the bed. "You are certainly welcome to carry on where you left off," he says as his eyes turn dark again. I slowly undo my jeans and peel them down my legs.

***

The following morning Vladimir, Cindy, and Porticus come over. Raphael calls the twins over and we all convene in the dining room. Raphael then explains about Regius, Bernadette, Harry, mine and his abilities, and Evangeline.

"You are kidding me?" says Vladimir.

"I really wish I was," Raphael says. I wish he was too. I miss Evangeline, well my Evangeline, the one that was completely fake.

"That's disgusting," says Porticus with a wrinkled nose.

"It is very appalling and we will deal with Evangeline in due course, but that is not the only issue we need to discuss. Some of you know that Mathias has left The Synod and has picked me to be the new leader," Raphael says.

"Woah, Mathias left? I never thought the old fart would ever leave!" says Lawrence. The others laugh.

"Can we please get back on track?" Raphael asks.

"Look Raph, we are all for you being the new leader if that's what you're worried about," says Porticus.

"As much as I do care about your opinions on that, I want to focus on the fact that there are now only three members. As it currently stands, The Synod is made up of myself, Vladimir, and Porticus. We need more members to make this work and to effectively reinvent The Synod. must ask, Porticus, why is Franklin not here?" he asks.

"He doesn't want to be involved." he says.

"That is perfectly fine. Now, Cindy, Lawrence, Nicholas, and Rosannah, you need to decide if you would like to be a member of The Synod and myself, Porticus and Vladimir, if we are happy for you to join. I am happy for all four of you to join," he says.

"I am happy with that," says Vladimir.

"As am I," says Porticus.

"We're definitely in," say the Twins together.

"You already know my answer," I smile.

"I can't turn down the chance to be a member of The Synod," says Cindy. So now The Synod now has seven members.

CHAPTER THIRTY-ONE

Raphael

"You are all aware of mine and Rosannah's ability to kill vampires. I must warn you now that betrayal of any kind *will* result in either Rosannah or myself ripping your heads off. I have faith in you, but it is essential that you understand this," I say.

"Can you both *really* kill vampires now?" Says Porticus.

"Yes, we can. You may see the bodies if you would like," I say.

"Yes, I'd like to," says Porticus.

"Very well, follow me," I say.

I lead everyone down into the crypt and open the coffins containing the corpses of Harry, Regius, and Bernadette. A smell emanates from the bodies and it is clear that they are beginning to decompose. Rosannah and Cindy's noses wrinkle up at the stench. The smell does not affect the rest of us. Rosannah and Cindy are new vampires, but us seasoned vampires are used to the smell of rotting flesh. I, along with the others, have seen many a rotting corpse during our time as vampires.

"How was it even possible to kill them?" asks Vladimir, pointing to the bodies.

"There is no explanation as to why Rosannah has the ability to, but I can because she changed me," I say.

"So dead vampires can actually rot?" Asks Porticus as he prods one of Bernadette's arms. He prods softly at first and then with a bit of force. He is able to push through the skin and flesh.

"It looks like it. I think it is very fascinating. The skin and flesh break down so that it can be eaten by insects I assume," I say.

"Urgh, can we leave the crypt now?" asks Cindy. "It actually smells pretty gross."

"I second that," says Rosannah who is now pinching her nose.

"Oh, yes. Of course," I say and close the coffins.

"Whatever the reasons, I'm happy that vampires can be killed. Something needs to control us and our numbers," says Porticus as we make our way out of the crypt and back to my dining room.

"I definitely agree. This is a great thing for vampires and you have no worries about me betraying you," says Vladimir.

"I agree too and there's no way I'd betray you," says Porticus.

"Same goes for us," say the Twins in unison.

"Me too," says Cindy.

"And me." Rosannah smiles.

"Now that is out of the way, I would like to discuss my newly acquired leadership. As you are aware Mathias left me as his successor. I would like to use this opportunity now to allow you to choose who you would like as your leader. You are The Synod and I feel it is your right to have a say in this. We will cast votes. Are you happy to say your nominations aloud or would you prefer to do it anonymously?" I ask.

"I think we should do this anonymously," says Vladimir.

"That is fine with me. I will sort out paper and a box. Please bear with me a few minutes." I race off, write a list of all of our names on seven pieces of paper, grab a box and head back.

"You may go into the hall one by one and circle your choice," I say as I hand out a list to each person. "Fold your paper four times and then put it into the box I am holding. I will then give it a shake and then read out the results."

We wait as each person takes their turn to go outside, cast their vote and return it to the box. My vote goes to Vladimir. The others are too new and I feel Vladimir would make a better leader than Porticus. After a small while all the votes are in the box.

"Does anyone have an issue with me reading out the results?" I ask just to make sure they are okay with it. Everyone nods their heads to show their agreement. Reaching into the box I pull out the first piece of paper. Unfolding it I read out the vote.

"Raphael," I read aloud and show everyone the paper. I read out and show the rest. Two are for Vladimir and the rest are for me. "So it would seem that I am your chosen leader by majority. If for any reason, I cannot fulfil my duty, I would like Vladimir to act in my place while I am indisposed. Is everyone happy with what has been decided today?" I ask and everyone nods happily. "Now that the leader issue is sorted we can now discuss the next matter. We are now seven. We each need to take on roles and responsibilities. I think the roles of welfare and female equality for vampires should be dropped. They are no longer as bigger an issue as they once were, although inequality in vampires was never an issue. Vampires aren't the same as humans, we do not think of the opposite sex as inferior in anyway. Annoying yes, inferior no."

"Then why did the role exist before?" Asks Rosannah narrowing her eyes at me.

"Because Mathias wanted to pander to *her*," I say and realisation dawns on Rosannah's face. "I have suggestions for each of you. Vladimir," I change the subject and turn to him. "I think you would be best suited to half of my old position, the unlawful killing of humans. Porticus, for you, illegal blood consumption. I know that it is the role you had originally wanted and I know you will give it the justice it deserves. Rosannah, for you the other half of my old role, the unlawful changing of humans."

"Thank you," she whispers with a smile.

"Cindy, for you, the role of lawfully changing humans." She smiles a huge grin at me. I think she must be very happy with my suggestion for her. "Lawrence, for you, intelligence and data gathering would be perfect because you want to know everyone's business and for you, Nicholas, Porticus's old role of security with the added element of secrecy. Are any of you not happy with my suggestions?" I ask.

"I am very happy with mine," says Rosannah.

"Me too," says Cindy.

"I'm pretty happy with mine," says Porticus.

"Yep, me too," says Vladimir.

"We're good too," Says Lawrence and Nicholas.

"Now for the last issue. Evangeline. What do we do about her?" I ask.

"I hate to say It, but I think we need to execute her. She had a major role in Rosannah being changed as well as a whole host of other crimes," says Lawrence.

"But look at what I did!" says Nicholas.

"You didn't kill or change anyone. You weren't involved in any of Evangeline's plans either. You were a really big douche, but you didn't actually break any rules. Plus, you've made up for it," says Lawrence.

"I agree," I say with a small smile.

"I agree with Lawrence about Evangeline," says Cindy.

"Me too," says Vladimir.

"And me," says Rosannah.

"There really shouldn't be anything to discuss. Evangeline has committed some pretty appalling crimes against vampires and The Synod. Harry, Reggie and Bernadette have already been executed," says Porticus.

"But those weren't decided beforehand. Harry was an accident and the other two were because of anger. If I hadn't of attacked Harry, we would never have known about my special ability," says Rosannah.

"Thank God you attacked him, imagine if you had finally had enough of us and even play fought with us thinking you wouldn't be able to actually hurt us," says Lawrence with a shiver.

"Rosannah, once we had all known about Harry we still would have decided that Reggie and Bernadette should have been executed. It's the same with Evangeline. Is there anyone who doesn't agree that death is what should be her punishment?" Porticus asks.

"You are right," I say reluctantly.

"Well that's the decision then. We will have to hunt her down and either you or Rosannah will kill her," says Porticus. There is no doubt about the punishment she deserves and how disgusted at her actions I am, but it will take a while to get my head around the fact that the sister I grew up with, loved and cared for, betrayed us the way she did. It does not matter that it turned out she was not blood related, it was her actions that stopped her being family.

"So it's decided. We find and execute Evangeline," says Vladimir. All the others agree with him.

"I think we should start to roll out the news of this new punishment too," says Porticus.

"No one is going to believe it," says Vladimir.

"If anyone wants proof they can come to my crypt. I have the bodies to prove it. I can even put them on display," I say.

"Raph, you and your trophies." Lawrencelaughs. Rosannah gives me a stern look and I give her a weak smile.

"I have not had any trophies for a number of years," I say feeling somewhat guilty.

"You've had trophies?" Rosannah asks incredulously.

"Let us not act like I am a saint," I say sadly.

"Yeah, because Raph is *far* from a saint. I know stories that will make your toes curl," says Lawrence.

"You are not helping *dear* brother," I say, narrowing my eyes at him.

"Oh right. Am I winding Rosannah up? Now that she doesn't go bright red I can't tell when she's mad or embarrassed for that matter," says Lawrence like he has no idea what he is doing. He knows *exactly* what he is doing!

"It's okay. I know that Raphael used to be somewhat evil, he is a vampire after all. Most probably go down the same route although there are exceptions right?" she asks everyone.

"There are not many. I've been there, Porticus has been there," says Vladimir regretfully.

"We've been there," says Nicholas.

"What are you talking about? Lawrence is still there, the evil wind up merchant!" Rosannah says. The twins laugh. "It's not even funny. You two should be ashamed of yourselves."

"Oh, I'm really ashamed," says Lawrence sarcastically but gives Rosannah a playful smile. A growl from me wipes the grin off his face.

"Let us get back to the matter at hand. How do we notify the vampire population about our ability to kill them?" I ask.

"I think you should start by giving Regius's wife her dead husband back. Bernadette can be delivered to any of her vampire friends. That will get the ball rolling," says Rosannah.

"That's a great idea, but what do we do with Harry's body?" Asks Nicholas.

"He can be ejected into space." Rosannah shrugs.

"Okay, so we can all put the feelers out and see if we can catch any news of Evangeline. I will deliver the bodies," I say.

"No Raph, Lawrence and I will do it," says Nicholas.

"And Porticus and I will eject Harry," says Vladimir.

"So we are all agreed?" I ask.

"Agreed," everyone says and they all race off out of my dining room, leaving Rosannah and I alone. Now the nerves really kick in.

CHAPTER THIRTY-TWO

Lawrence

After leaving Raphael's house, Nicholas and I head down into the crypt with Vladimir and Porticus. I open the relevant coffins.

"Are you two going to be okay taking a body each?" asks Vladimir.

"I think we'll do this a body at a time," says Nicholas. While looking at Harry's head, a crazy idea enters mine.

"Hey, check this out," I say as I take Harry's head and throw it into the air. As it comes down I kick it down the aisle as hard as I can. We all watch as it flies at a wall. Some of the flesh on Harry's head breaks up and splatters everywhere while the skull itself causes a crater in the wall. "Oh shit," I exclaim.

"*You* can explain that to Raphael," says Nicholas.

"Damn, he's definitely gonna kill you now!" Vladimir laughs.

"Do you really think so?" I ask nervously.

"Well no, but he may remove some of your limbs," jokes Nicholas.

"Way to make me feel better."

"Look Lawrence, it was an accident, you'll be fine," says Nicholas.

"Sorry to love and leave you, but we need to get this show on the road," says Porticus who takes

Harry's body and flings it over his shoulder. Vladimir picks up Harry's battered head and they dash off.

"Seriously Lawrence, what were you thinking?" asks Nicholas with a serious expression.

"I don't know, but it was pretty cool huh?" I ask.

"Oh hell yes!" Nicholas laughs and gives me a high five. Looking back at the remaining bodies I'm unsure what one to go for first, but something tells me that Bernadette is probably best.

"I say we go for Bernadette first," says Nicholas, reading my mind.

"Excellent, shotgun!" I yell and Nicholas rolls his eyes at me before grabbing Bernadette's body and throwing it over his right shoulder. One of the main differences between us is that I'm right handed and he's left.

Nicholas gives me a look of complete distain.

"Oh come on, don't act like you've never wanted Bernadette draped over your body," I say.

"For starters, I prefer any woman who's draped over me to be alive and naked. Secondly, I have NEVER wanted to sleep with Bernadette, she's vile. And thirdly, I'm in love with Brianna, "he states.

"Wow, you're a bit touchy aren't you," I say.

"Look at what's on my fucking shoulder! Can you just grab the bitch's arms and legs and we can get this over and done with? We've got Reggie to do next," he yells.

"I'd swear you've got a sudden case of PMS. With all these revelations recently it seems anything is possible," I say as I close the coffin containing Reggie. I grab Bernadette's limbs and head and Nicholas rolls his eyes again.

We race off to where Bernadette lives and after breaking into her house we head for her telephone. Most people keep their address book by the telephone and fortunately for us, so did Bernadette. Nicholas dumps Bernadette into an arm chair and I chuck the parts I'm holding on to too.

"Make sure you keep a hold of those, we wouldn't want you to lose any part of yourself would we?" I joke to her and then walk over to the address book. Looking through the various people I recognise a few of the names, but one stands out more than all of the others, *Claudia Sherman*. Pain stabs at my chest, but I try to push it away. How could she possibly know Bernadette? I mean, pretty much all vampires know of The Synod, but not all of them know The Synod personally. The entry is pretty old so it looks like they've known each other for some time. Claudia never mentioned this, but then again, she was very good at keeping secrets. I go to turn the page but Nicholas stops me.

"That looks like a great candidate," he says.

"I don't think so," I say, hoping he will take the bait.

"Why not, they're as good as any," he says.

"Nicholas, look at the name," I urge him.

"It's a *Claudia Sherman*, what's with... Oooooooh," he says as realisation dawns on him. "You think that's *her*?"

"She lives at the same address; it has to be her," I say with a heavy sigh.

"Well then, she's definitely the one we want to drop Bernadette off to. She bloody deserves it!" Says Nicholas.

"I don't think this is a good idea," I say.

"This is your opportunity to get some kind of payback on the bitch. If you don't do this, I will!" he says. I know he means business and out of the two of us, I'd rather I did this.

"Alright, alright. Can you wait here while I go to see her?" I ask.

"Yeah, sure," he says.

"I'll call you when I'm ready to show Claudia the body," I say. He nods and I race off arriving at her front door in minutes. She opens it before I can knock. Her eyes clap onto mine and she smiles widely with surprised recognition. The last time I saw her was fifteen years ago.

"Oh Lawrence, it's been ages. How are you? Please come in," she says and steps back to let me in. Giving her a weak smile I step inside and she closes the door behind me. She shows me to her front room and I take a seat. She sits opposite me and smiles warmly at me again. I have the most uncomfortable feeling being sat here. This is the woman who took my heart and put it through a blender and then poured vinegar on the wounds of where my heart was and this is the very place it happened.

Claudia and I were in a relationship for six months. I was prowling for a human to drink from at a bar when I caught sight of a tall, leggy blonde with bright blue eyes. In that instance, I knew she was the one. I fell in love with her instantaneously. I approached her and as soon as she looked at me her crystals blues turned black and I knew I'd had a deep effect on her. We dated for a while and it wasn't long before we became a couple and she gave me a key to her house.

On the instructions of Claudia was I didn't tell anyone about our relationship, although Nicholas had guessed I was seeing someone. Claudia and I were meant to be madly in love, but it was still early days and Claudia wanted to wait until we were ready to tell anyone. I went along with it because I thought I had found my soul mate.

Everything was going fine until I went away. I went to Africa with Nicholas to have a lad's holiday. I was meant to be gone for a week, but I was missing Claudia like crazy. Before I'd left she'd told me how much she was going to miss me and that she didn't know what she'd do with herself while I was gone, so I thought it would be a nice to cut the trip short and surprise her by turning up at her house unannounced. I expected to find my beautiful, caring and lovesick girlfriend so happy to see me. What I found instead was her in bed having a threesome with two human guys on the bed we had made love on so many times. She was having a wail of a time that she hadn't even realised I'd entered her home and was standing in her bedroom watching these guys fuck her until I let out a huge growl. Needless to say I discovered in those mere minutes why Claudia was so happy to keep our relationship a secret. Goodness knows how many other people she had been fucking behind my back. I was beyond seething and I was crushed. Claudia tried to explain that she had a thing for humans, but I didn't care. She had ruined something that was meant to be sacred.

They were the last human beings that I'd killed that weren't criminals. After I had ripped them apart, I went home covered in their blood and flesh. Nicholas was pretty shocked when he saw me, but he was my saviour. I was ready to go to The Synod and tell them what I'd done so they could eject me into space, but fortunately Nicholas talked me out of it. After he got all of the details out of me he got me tidied up and whisked me back to Africa and took me on a world tour so that I could have some time to sort myself out. I was incredibly dubious, but it actually worked and when we came back eight months later I was much better than I was, but I vowed never to fall in love again.

Nicholas and I have kept the deaths a secret ever since as well as mine and Claudia's relationship. As far as anyone else is concerned, Nicholas and I had a wild trip, drinking and fucking our way around the world, visiting every country on our way. It looks like Claudia kept the deaths a secret too because we have never heard anything since.

"Why have you come to see me?" Claudia laughs pulling me from my thoughts. I try my best not to look at her in disgust.

"I'm not here for a good reason. I am here to tell you some pretty awful news."

"Oh?" she asks with worry.

"I am aware that you know Bernadette," I say.

"Oh yes." She smiles.

"I will start by telling you that she has committed some terrible crimes against The Synod," I say. Claudia's face drops.

"Has she been sentenced to be ejected into space?" She asks. She doesn't appear to be very concerned about Bernadette.

"No," I say.

"Oh. But wait, didn't you say you had some bad news for me?" she asks.

"Yes, I do. I need you to do something for me first. I need you to have an open mind. What I'm about to tell you will come as a pretty big shock okay?"

"Okay," she agrees.

"Bernadette is dead; she has been executed." I say. Claudia's face scrunches up in confusion.

"Vampires can't be killed."

"They can now. My brother and his girlfriend can kill vampires," I say.

"You must be lying!" she yells. "I know we didn't break up on the best of terms but you coming here and telling me such shit is unbelievable. Please leave!"

"I actually have proof. I am not only here to tell you about Bernadette's death, but to also deliver her body," I say.

"Body?" she asks.

"Yes, can I bring her to you?" I ask.

"Yes, but if this is some joke..."

"It really isn't," I say and call Nicholas.

"You can bring her here now," I say down the line.

"Okay, but I'm going to do it in two trips," he says and hangs up.

In minutes he arrives and Claudia answers the door.

"What? No way. Lawrence, you never told me that you were a twin," she says as she shows Nicholas in. He's holding Bernadette's torso and is looking at Claudia with scrutiny. He's wondering what I saw in her. Another difference between us is that we have completely different tastes in women. I can tell already by the way he's looking at her that he doesn't think she's attractive.

"I told you I had two brothers," I say.

"Yeah but not that one was an identical twin," she says eyeing Nicholas up. He looks her up and down with disgust and drops the torso at her feet. She jumps back a little as Nicholas races off. "You know; this could be anybody's torso."

"Hold on for a minute, Nicholas is bringing the rest of her," I say. After a few minutes he arrives with her arms, legs and head.

"Oh my God, it really is Bernadette!" she says with shock as she takes the head from Nicholas. "She really is dead!" She says incredulously. She still doesn't appear to be very upset.

"Yes, I am very sorry for your loss," I say sarcastically. "But please know that her crimes involve being part of a group who plotted and carried out the unlawful changing of two humans as well as actively seeking to kill one of them beforehand."

"What's going to happen to the rest of the group?" She asks.

"Two of them have been killed and the other is on the run," I say.

"How is this even possible?" she asks.

"Like I said, my brother and his girlfriend are capable of killing vampires," I say deadpan.

"So after all this time the only reason you come to see me is to deliver a dead vampire?" she asks in disbelief.

"Yes, I have had no desire to see you since the last time I saw you."

"Really?" she asks.

"You're kidding right?" asks Nicholas. "You seriously wonder why Lawrence hasn't wanted to see you all this time? It's because you were a dirty, skanky hoe," he says. Claudia's jaw drops.

"Thank you brother," I say sarcastically.

"Anytime bro," he says glaring at Claudia. One thing that still bugs me is how she knew Bernadette.

"How the heck did you even know Bernadette?" I ask.

"I wasn't mean to say anything but it makes no difference now. She created me about thirty years ago. She didn't want anyone to know because she could get into big trouble."

Bernadette actually *made* a vampire? All those times I'd overheard her spouting her mouth off about how she would never change a human to a vampire because most humans didn't deserve it in her eyes and she was the one who created Claudia? Mind boggled.

"Why did Bernadette change you?" I ask.

"I knew a vampire called Evangeline who I'd asked to change me, but she was quite funny about the idea so she got Bernadette to do it as a favour. After I was changed, Evangeline stopped being my friend," she says. Holy fuck, is there anything Evangeline hasn't been a part of!?

"Look, this has been great and all but I'm covered in this filthy scum. Can we get going now please?" asks an exasperated Nicholas.

"Yeah, we have another body to drop off," I say and we turn to leave.

"Lawrence!" Claudia yells after me. I turn to see what she wants. "What am I supposed to do with Bernadette?" she asks.

"You can start by showing her to every vampire you know, then you can tell them what she did and who killed her," I say and Nicolas and I race back off to the crypt.

CHAPTER THIRTY-THREE

Nicholas

We arrive back the crypt and I eye up the damage Lawrence caused earlier.

"I still can't believe you did that," I say.

"Come on, you know me. I'm always fun and games," he smiles. Damn that fucking bitch Claudia. She almost killed my brother, but thank God he made a recovery and can be himself these days. Did I think it was a good idea to see her? Probably not, but I hope Lawrence got some kind of retribution by me dumping Bernadette at her feet.

"Yeah I do know you, but I also know our older brother can actually kill you now."

"I won't tell him about it unless Rosannah is there," he says.

"Hiding behind a girl." I laugh.

"A girl who can also kill me, but has the strength to stop Raphael if he goes all *let's kill Lawrence*."

"Do you really think he'll kill you?" I ask, wondering if my brother is actually worried.

"Not intentionally, but he's used to being violent with me, with us. All it takes is for him to forget that he's all super-duper and that's the end," he says. He has a point, maybe Rosannah being there when he tells him isn't such a bad idea.

Lawrence opens the coffin containing Reggie and pulls out the bag filled with his corpse.

"Don't play ball with his head, we're going to need it to prove this mess is actually Reggie," I say.

"No worries, you can carry him to make sure I don't do anything stupid," he says with a smile. I just walked straight into that.

Lawrence seals the coffin and we race off to Reggie's house. We have to knock on the door to get an answer. Reggie's wife is a vampire but she never answers the door unless someone knocks. The door opens and she eyes us up with suspicion.

"Reggie isn't here," she says.

"We know, that's why we're here," I say.

"Can we come in, we need to talk to you about him," says Lawrence. She walks off into the front room and we take that as an invitation to come in. We follow her into the kitchen.

"That bag you've got there stinks, why on Earth have you got a dead body with you?" she asks.

"You've probably been wondering where Reggie is," says Lawrence.

"He disappears all the time, I gave up wondering hundreds of years ago, but you said you have something to tell me about him," she says.

"Yes, the body in the bag is Reggie," I say and drop the bag on the kitchen floor. She raises her eyebrows and opens the bag.

"Huh, so death finally caught up with him. How the hell did this happen?" she asks. Two things strike me as very odd. One: she isn't upset that her husband is dead. Two: she isn't shocked that vampires can be killed.

"Aren't you at all surprised?" asks Lawrence, reading my mind.

"If you had told me that Reggie was dead before I saw the body I wouldn't have believed you until I saw him, but having seen the body first I have no choice but to believe he's dead. I have been around for so long what's the point in standing here in awe?"

"Would you at least like to know how and why he died?" I ask astounded.

"Yeah, I suppose that would be nice," she says.

"He committed crimes against The Synod and humans. My brother and his girlfriend have the ability to kill vampires. It was my brother's girlfriend who killed Reggie," I explain. Something flickers behind her eyes, but whatever it is has gone in seconds.

"You are free to tell whichever vampires you want about this, but I'd advise you show them Reggie's corpse to prove you're telling the truth. The vampires that have found so far have been quite surprised by this new revelation and have needed proof to believe it," says Lawrence.

"Certainly," she says and picks up the bag. "Thank you for bringing Reggie to me, I've got quite a few vampires to tell about this. You can see yourselves out," she smiles and wanders off upstairs. Lawrence and I look at each other and then shrug. We head back to Lawrence's house to clean up. Once we are done we head over to Raphael's.

He opens the door as we arrive and Rosannah is soon by his side.

"We have some good news and bad news," admits Lawrence as we all head into the kitchen.

"I will take the bad news first," says Raphael.

"Good news? What a great choice, I'll tell you that first," says Lawrence. Raphael growls so I jump in.

"We delivered Bernadette to one of her friends. This particular friend turned out to be a creation of Bernadette," I say. Raphael's eyebrows shoot up.

"Bernadette was so anti-changing any humans herself but one exists? How curious," he says scratching his chin.

"Yes, we found out the reason why Bernadette was so anti-changing, it was because she changed this woman in secret. She would have been in serious trouble and so her being anti appears to be a cover," Lawrence says.

"You want to know what's even more curious than that? The woman knew Evangeline and wanted to become a vampire. Evangeline refused to change her, but pulled in a favour from Bernadette, I say. Raphael growls lightly and Rosannah threads an arm around his waist. If Lawrence wants to tell Raphael about the crypt, now is probably the best time. As if reading my mind Lawrence clears his throat.

"Now for the, err, bad news. I may or may not have taken Harry's head and I may or may not have kicked it around your crypt and damaged one of the walls," he says. Raphael races off and comes back within minutes. Raphael's eyes are pitch black and Rosannah rushes to his side.

"What did you do to my crypt?!" he yells and goes to grab Lawrence but Rosannah pulls him back.

"Come on Raph, it was an accident, I had no idea it was going to do any damage," Lawrence says, slowly backing away from Raphael.

"It was a *vampire's* head; it was clear it wasn't going to shatter like a human skull! A marble wall verses a vampire skull, the weaker substance is going to take the brunt of the force!" Raphael yells as he tries to get closer to Lawrence.

"Look Raph, forgive me, but I've never had the opportunity to kick a detached vampire head before!" yells Lawrence. Raphael lets out a huge roar and jumps forward taking Rosannah with him. Rosannah corrects herself and Lawrence jumps over to me and then to the kitchen door just in time.

"Raphael, stop. You can really kill him you know!" she yells pulling him back again.

"What do you think I am trying to do!" he yells trying to pull forward again.

"Raphael, to be fair you can always get the crypt fixed you know," I say trying to defuse the situation.

"You are right," Raphael says.

"You two best go for now," says Rosannah. Lawrence and I take the hint and dash off passing Vladimir and Porticus on our way.

CHAPTER THIRTY-FOUR

Raphael

"I cannot believe him!" I say through gritted teeth as Vladimir and Porticus walk into the kitchen.

"Ah, so Lawrence lives another day!" jokes Porticus.

"Only just," says Rosannah with her arms still around me. Porticus and Vladimir watch in amusement.

"You can let go of me now. I am not going to run after him and kill him," I say to her.

"Are you sure?" she asks with a raised eyebrow.

"Yes," I say smiling. God, what would I do without this woman? A woman who is capable of holding me back when I need it. She lets go of me and places a kiss on my lips. A very peculiar thought occurs to me as I look into her eyes. Why has it not come to me before?

"Raph, we've come to tell you that Harry has been ejected into space, but we showed him around to a lot of vampires we know. The news is probably spreading like wild fire now," says Vladimir.

"That is great. The more vampires that know about this the better," I say.

"So what do we do from here?" asks Porticus.

"We just carry on as normal until we hear about Evangeline," I say.

"So no monthly meetings?" Asks Vladimir.

"There is no need to. We can contact and see each other whenever we need to," I say.

"Okay, we'll be in touch if we hear anything," says Porticus.

"Likewise," I say and they dash off leaving me back to my thoughts and Rosannah.

"I have something I need to do and I do not want you seeing. Can you go out for a while?" I ask. Rosannah looks at me suspiciously, but dashes out of the front door anyway.

I race upstairs wondering if I have lost my mind. When I realised I was in love with Rosannah I knew that I wanted her forever. When she became mine forever I wanted more, I wanted her to live with me. Once she moved in and started sharing my home I should have been satisfied with that and I was, but now I am not. I still want more. I want, need, for her to have my name.

I enter my room and a barrage of thoughts race through my mind. What kind of proposal would Rosannah want? Would she even want to marry me? Would my brothers love her as a sister in law? Is now really the time to ask her? Oh for God's sake man! Just get a grip of yourself! Think about it, what do you need? Candles, you need candles. I race back downstairs and into the kitchen. I grab my whole supply of candles and race back upstairs to my room. I place them around strategically around and light them. I walk back down the stairs and start to pace.

"Reow," Marmalade meows at me. I turn to her and she walks over to me. I bend down and scratch under her chin. She purrs lightly and rubs the sides of her face against my hand.

"Oh Marmalade, I want to ask your mummy to marry me and all I have is candles. What if that is not enough?" I ask her. She carries on and then it hits me. "Oh damn it! How could I possibly forget that!?" I shout, startling Marmalade. I race to my study and punch in the code to my safe. Reaching into the back I pull out a very old small wooden box. My hand shakes as I look at it. It contains a ring that I never thought I would ever look at again. Nor did I think anyone would even wear it again. Steeling myself I open the box to reveal my mother's wedding and engagement rings. As the eldest son I inherited everything and although I divided most things out, I kept these much to the dislike of Evangeline. Lawrence has our father's wedding ring. I take my mother's engagement ring out and take a good look at it. I have not seen this ring since I took it off of my mother's dead hand. The ring is beautiful, just as she was. It is a thick patterned gold band with a large rectangular cut diamond with round diamonds either side that graduate in size as they travel down the sides. Judging the band and my memory of Rosannah's fingers, this should fit her perfectly.

I place the wedding ring back into the safe and lock it back up. I race back upstairs cradling the ring box in my hand. I put it into my pocket and wait nervously until Rosannah returns.

"What is this?" she asks as she walks into our bedroom. Candles flicker around the room and I walk over to Rosannah and take her hands in mine.

"Rosannah, you know that I love you with every essence of my being. I was petrified I would lose you,

I thought I actually had lost you. Now I have you forever," I say mumbling and bumbling.

"You're being really soppy, is everything okay?" Rosannah asks. I sigh and drop to one knee. Rosannah's eyes widen. I swallow the lump that appears to have formed in my throat and continue.

"Rosannah, I know that now is not the best time and I know I should have waited, but I do not want to wait any more. I want you to be my wife, to carry my name. Will you marry me?" I ask and produce the little wooden box. Opening it, I reveal my mother's ring. "I want you to have this, to wear it forever. It was my mother's engagement ring." Rosannah puts her hands to her face and starts to cry. I am not sure that this is the kind of reaction I wanted. I was hoping for happiness. Rosannah removes her hands and looks at the ring.

"Yes, yes I'll marry you!" she screams and holds out her left hand. I slip the ring onto her finger, it fits perfectly just like I knew it would. I stand up and take her in my arms. "You have made me the happiest vampire in the world!" I say and kiss her.

"We have to tell my mum about this you know. You can change your mind if you want."

"Not a chance," I reply.

CHAPTER THIRTY-FIVE

Evangeline

"You've got me to come all the way to Germany and so far I know nothing of your plan. Are you going to tell me at some point?" They ask.

"You say it like I made you come here. You came here of your own free will with barely any information. I think that says more about you than it does about me," I say.

"Well I'm here now and I'd like to know what this plan of yours is"they say.

"Such impatience, but I shall tell you. We both know that Rosannah can no longer be a direct target so I propose this: first we eliminate the best friend, then the mother. And any other human that means anything to her will be targets. Just because I can't kill her physically doesn't mean I can't mentally and emotionally. She must pay for what she has done in any way possible!" I yell.

"Bitter much?" They ask.

"You don't know the half of it!" I yell.

"So when are we going to get started?"

"Quite eager aren't you?" I ask with glee. I knew that they would be the perfect choice to recruit on my crusade. "I don't care about any vendettas you may have against them, I have my own to deal with," they say.

"And I don't care about yours as long as you do what you are told," I say.

"You have no worries about that, just tell me what and when and I'm there," they say.

"I'll let things settle down first, let them fall into a lull of false security and then when they least expect it we will strike," I say with a huge grin.

"The news that they are able to kill vampires is spreading, aren't worried about that at all?" they ask.

"There's no way they'd kill me, I'm family! They had the perfect opportunity and they let me go!" I say. "And as for you, they'll never even suspect you." I laugh.

ABOUT THE AUTHOR

Taniquelle Tulipano is an adult romance author who resides in London, England with her husband and daughter.

For updates and to find out more visit:
www.taniquelletulipano.com
www.facebook.com/taniquelletulipano

BOOKS BY TANIQUELLE TULIPANO

The Monstrum Vampire Series

Dead Beginnings (Monstrum #1)
The Lost Brother (Monstrum #2)
Princess of the Dark (Monstrum #3)

18872117R00121

Printed in Great Britain
by Amazon